Blitzed

Robert Swindells

One night in 1940 they bombed Bradford. I was there, but I remember nothing about it. I slept through the whole thing, in a clothes-basket, in the air-raid shelter my mum shared with the people next door. I was seventeen months old.

By the time I was eleven, I'd got really interested in World War Two – especially the aeroplanes. My mum told me about the raid I'd slept through, and I started wishing I'd been older so I could hear the explosions, see the fires. Only exciting thing to happen in my flipping lifetime, and I'd gone and missed it.

I joined the RAF at seventeen, and was posted to Germany. One evening a friend, Gisela, invited me home to meet her folks. Her dad asked whereabouts in England I was from. Bradford, I told him. Ah, he smiled. I used to fly over Bradford on my way to bomb Manchester and Liverpool.

Weird, or what? Back then, I was a baby and this guy was the enemy. He might easily have blown me to bits, while *our* fliers were dropping bombs on kids like Gisela. Now, thirteen years later we were laughing together, eating cake and drinking coffee in his home. Afterwards I thought, *why couldn't we have left out the bombing, cut straight to the coffee and cake?*

Blitzed is aimed at those thousands of kids who seem fascinated by the Second World War, even today. At the core of it lie Miss Coverley's words to Georgie's classmates: *war is mostly sad*.

Down with bombs. Up with coffee and cake!

From the Carnegie Medal-winning author

ROBERT SWINDELLS

Blitzed

www.heinemann.co.uk

✓ Free online support
✓ Useful weblinks
✓ 24 hour online ordering

01865 888080

Heinemann is an imprint of Pearson Education Limited, a company
incorporated in England and Wales, having its registered office at
Edinburgh Gate, Harlow, Essex, CM20 2JE.
Registered company number: 872828

Heinemann is the registered trademark of
Pearson Education Limited

© Robert Swindells, 2002
First published in Great Britain in 2002 by Doubleday,
an imprint of Random House Children's Books

First published in the New Windmills Series in 2008

Activities by David Grant

Activities © Pearson Education Limited 2008

12 11 10 09 08
10 9 8 7 6 5 4 3 2 1

British Library Cataloguing in Publication Data is available from the British
Library on request.

13-digit ISBN: 978-0-435-13198-2

Typeset by Phoenix Photosetting, Chatham, Kent
Printed in China by CTPS Ltd

Acknowledgements

Every effort has been made to contact copyright holders of material reproduced
in this book. Any omissions will be rectified in subsequent printings if notice is
given to the publishers.
Short extract from Winston Churchill's speech broadcast on 27th April, 1941.
Reprinted with permission of Curtis Brown Limited, London.

My thanks to Richard Marriott, Sheila Gijsen and Arthur Arnold for help with research.

One

'Dad, what if the Queen trumped on telly?'

'*George!*' goes Mum, before Dad has a chance to answer. Emily gets the giggles. She's seven, thinks trump's the ultimate swearword. The six o'clock news is on. State opening of Parliament. I only ask 'cause I'm bored. Anything's better than boredom, even getting shouted at, but Dad doesn't shout. Knows me too well, I suppose. Instead he's like, 'Never happen, old lad, they're trained to avoid stuff like that: starts when they're two.' Comes out with it deadpan, like it's common knowledge, eyes never leave the screen.

'Oh,' I reply. Well, what else can I say? Emily's still giggling. She's got her hands over her face so Mum can't zap her with a frown. I get up. 'Off to my room.' Nobody begs me to stay.

Best bit of the house, my room. Done out in a World War Two theme. Mum's forever moaning about my models. Dust traps, she calls them. Military vehicles is what they actually are. I've got fourteen so far, built 'em all myself. From kits. Tanks, scout cars, trucks. I've got seventeen planes as well, hanging from the ceiling; all World War Two. I don't collect any other sort.

I lie on my bed and look up at the planes. The Stuka's my favourite, it's a dive-bomber. *Was*, I mean, in the war. I've hung it so it looks as if it's diving straight at me. It's really ugly, like an iron vulture. I think that's why I like it.

I can't wait till tomorrow. We're off up to Yorkshire, to this World War Two museum. Eden Camp. It's called that because it used to be a prisoner-of-war camp, and I know what you're thinking. You're thinking, *Yawn yawn, flipping museum*, but it's not *that* sort of museum. Dad got a brochure and it looks cool. Really cool. Anyway I don't give a toss what you think – it's not you who's *going*, is it?

Two

Seven o'clock. Breakfast. I look at Dad. 'What time we setting off, Dad?'

He eyeballs me over his coffee mug. 'You're lucky to be setting off at *all*, lad, that crack about the Queen.'

'What? It wasn't a crack, it was a question.'

'Same thing, question like that.'

'Trump,' murmurs Emily.

'And that'll do from *you* as well, young woman.'

We get off at half eight. One hour drive. Mum up front, me and Em in the back. Brilliant weather, loads of traffic. 'Hope they're not all going where we're going,' says Mum.

Dad shakes his head. 'East coast, most of 'em. Scarborough, Brid. Not many people go to museums.'

'They're trained to avoid stuff like that,' I can't resist saying. 'Starts when they're two.' He looks at me in the mirror but I'm deadpan, gazing out the window. He doesn't say anything.

Eden Camp's even acer than I expected. First thing I see is this Hurricane: real one, parked in the open. Tank, too. And then the huts: rows of 'em, each one dedicated to a different aspect of World War Two. We're two and a half hours going through them all. One's all about evacuation: thousands of kids with labels on like parcels, getting on trains to go and live in the countryside where they won't be bombed. 'How would you fancy *that*, you two?' goes Mum. 'Say goodbye to me and your dad, go off to live in some stranger's house with no idea how long it's going to last?'

Em shakes her head and slips her hand through Mum's arm, but I grin. 'It'd be great: somewhere different, new stuff to do, no school.'

'They'd have to go to *school*, dummy,' goes Dad. '*Strange* schools too, full of kids they didn't know and teachers who didn't want 'em there, probably. And no mum to run home to if you didn't like it.'

'I wouldn't care: at least I wouldn't be *bored* all the time like I am now.'

He has no answer to that. We move on.

One hut has a doodlebug outside it, mounted on a plinth. The doodlebug was this flying bomb with a jet engine and a ton of high explosive in its nose. The Germans invented it; they were cleverer than us in the war. 'Its *real* name was the V-1,' I say to Emily. She's fed up and doesn't give a hoot if its real name was Z-50,000, but I've read all about the V-1 and want to show off. 'It flew at five hundred miles an hour and could wipe out a whole street of houses. The way it worked was—'

'I don't think your sister's particularly interested in flying bombs, Georgie,' goes Mum, taking Em's hand. 'Come on, sweetheart, I know where there's some lovely ice-cream.'

Ice-cream? What's ice-cream got to do with World War Two, that's what I'd like to know.

We all have some, then we come to the best hut of all: the Blitz hut. It's absolutely unbelievable: dark and smoky with the drone of enemy bombers overhead, bombs whistling down, bangs and flashes of anti-aircraft guns and a pulsating glow from burning buildings. It's not real, of course, but they've made a fantastic job of faking it. Right at the far end is this bombed-out house: drifts of smashed bricks and rubble with bits of furniture and stuff sticking out and water spurting from a fractured pipe. It's like you're *there*, in London, in the autumn of 1940.

There's a barrier. I lean on it for ages, watching and listening. And wishing. The others have moved on and I don't notice till Dad comes back and taps me on the shoulder, making me jump. 'Come on, Georgie, we wondered where on earth you'd got to.'

I follow him out, my ears ringing. 'Dad, I wish . . .'

'What?'

'I wish I'd been there. Seen it all. It must've been dead exciting.'

He shakes his head. 'Awful, old lad. People blown to bits, cut to ribbons by flying glass. Imagine Emily buried under tons of rubble, all by herself, choking. They don't show the full horror.'

Mum catches the tail-end of this and says, 'Ask Miss Coverley at number twenty-two, Georgie: she was in London, she'll tell you.'

Which just goes to show how much mums know. Miss Coverley doesn't like me and I don't like her. I wouldn't ask her for a bucket of water if I was on fire, the miserable old bag. I can't be bothered now 'cause I'm knackered, but I'll tell you all about Miss Coverley tomorrow.

Something for you to look forward to.

Three

Sunday I phone Pete before I go downstairs. He's like, 'Uugh . . . hello, who is it? Whaddya want?' Old Pete. Sleeps like the dead, takes about five hours to come round. I could've called Daniel but it's more fun with Pete.

'Georgie,' I shout. 'Who d' you *think*?'

'Gnuuuh. *Time* is it, you moron?'

'Four a.m.'

'You're *kidding*.'

''Course I am. It's half-past eight, sun's burning your eyeballs out, get *up*.'

'Hunnh . . . gimme half-hour, right?'

'Right. Nine, usual place. And call Danny.'

I grab a coffee, jog along to Sparrow Park. It isn't a park, just a triangle of grass with doggie-poo, four trees and a bench. We hang out there, Pete, Danny and me. I'm first, so to pass the time I rig up an invisible machine-gun and blaze away at some Nazi tanks clanking up Cardigan Road. I'm so into it I don't hear Pete and Danny till Danny says, ''S right, Sergeant, give 'em hell.'

'Oh, hi.' I cease firing, act like I'm not embarrassed at all. They know I'm mad on World War Two.

'So,' goes Pete, 'how was it?'

'Ace.' I've brought the leaflet. I open it, they join me on the bench. 'All these huts, see? Twenty-nine of 'em, each on a different topic.' I read a few out. '"The Rise of Hitler". "Britain Prepares". "Women at War". But *this* is the best.' I point to hut 5. '"Blitz". I'm not kidding: it feels like you're *there*.'

'Hmm: wouldn't mind a bit of that myself.'

'Old Coverley was in the Blitz, y'know.'

'Got *her* in hut 5, have they?' goes Pete. Danny laughs.

'Yeah,' I say. 'In a glass case.'

'And I bet she's got her gardening stuff with her, right: little fork, ball of twine, beat-up kneeling mat?'

''Course. Got her flipping *garden* in there as well: only way they could get her to stay.' You should see the old bag's garden, she spends her *life* grubbing about in it.

We horse around a bit, then Danny says, 'Talking about old Coverley, why don't we creep the backs, mess up some flowerbeds?'

Creeping's when you streak across a row of back gardens, over fences, through hedges, across veg patches. It's brilliant. You've got to be quick so you don't get caught or recognised. If some sad geezer recognises you he'll rat on you to your folks and you'll get grounded. We usually do the even side of Cardigan Road: the side I don't live on and Coverley does. The Sandersons at twenty-six have a nasty dog, part German shepherd, part shark. That adds to the general excitement, I can tell you.

When you live in a dump like Witchfield, you've got to make your own entertainment.

Four

We stroll along Cardigan Road trying to look like we've been to church, and turn into the snicket that runs up the side of number twenty. This block of seven houses is our all-time favourite creeping course. Seven back gardens means eight dividers, which can be walls, fences of various sorts, or hedges. On this creep we're looking at a six-foot wall, a privet hedge, a picket fence, two five foot walls with the Sanderson dog between 'em, two woven fences and another six foot wall. Beyond that wall is a snicket like the one we're loitering in. If we reach it safely we'll stroll back onto Cardigan and saunter off as if nothing's happened. Sounds easy and we've done it loads of times before, but with creeping it depends *when* you do it. The easiest time, not counting three in the morning, is on a dark winter evening when doors are locked and curtains are drawn and everybody's gawping at the telly. It's so simple then that it's nearly as boring as maths homework. Winter's pretty easy even in broad daylight, unless there's deep snow. Spring and autumn are dodgier because people might have their doors open, and somebody's practically bound to be pottering about in the garden instead of getting a flipping life. But the most dangerous time of all is a Sunday in summer. Like today.

Pete goes 'Now' and we're off. I always play I'm escaping from a prisoner-of-war camp, running for the wire between sweeps of the searchlight, knowing I've got to clear the fence and reach the woods before the sentries spot me from their towers and open up with machine-guns. *Killed while trying to escape.*

Number twenty's a doddle. Door closed, nice flat lawn, thin spot in the privet where we've crashed through lots of times. Once through the hedge we're in Miss Coverley's. 'Watch it!' yells Pete, wading through a stand of dahlias. The door's wide open and I see the old bag through my eye corner, waddling across the carpet in her threadbare slippers.

'*I know you!*' she screeches, as me and Danny plunge through, decapitating dahlias all the way. '*I know where you live, I'll tell your dad what you get up to, see if I don't.*' She's got to be talking to me: the others live miles away.

The picket fence sways as we scramble over, laughing like madmen. Twenty-four's got something under those pointy glass things: cloches, I think they're called. Pete sticks his foot through one by accident, and it's a good job our trainers have thick soles 'cause the cloches smash dead easy and there's broken glass everywhere, *really* hazardous. You'd think people'd *think* about that, wouldn't you?

Luckily our Nikes save us and here's the wall with the dog behind it. It's been barking like a lunatic since the glass broke, but it sounds as if it's inside. Not that *that* guarantees us a safe crossing of the Sanderson ranch, because Sanderson's a psychopath. Last summer he opened the door and told his ugly land-shark to get us, just because some rotten tomato plants had got in our way. *Sane* person wants tomatoes he goes down Sainsbury's, right?

We top the wall and I can't believe it: he's only got tomatoes in exactly the same spot, which *proves* he's a nutter. So it's two crop failures in two years and he must be out, because there's old Jaws hurling himself against the sliding door, barking to wake the dead and nobody comes.

We take our time over the next wall, beginning to relax. Only a couple of woven fences now between us and the final barrier. Never go in for woven fencing, by the way: it splits really easily when it's old. Goes brittle. We jog across the last three gardens, leaving wafers of the stuff strewn across paths and lawns. Amazingly there's nobody about: maybe they're churchgoers. We sit astride the wall, looking back, feeling a sense of anticlimax. The dog's still going ballistic behind the double glazing and old Coverley's gawping short-sightedly in our direction, otherwise it's quiet. 'There ought to be towers,' I growl. 'You know: watchtowers with searchlights and machine-guns.'

We climb down and trudge back to Sparrow Park. Four old guys are sitting on our bench. I roll an invisible grenade under it and blow them to bits. We sit in Wendy's slurping Coke. I don't know how we stand the excitement.

Five

Something good happens Monday, though, and *that's* got to be a first. I mean *Monday*, five school days stretching endlessly in front of you. Sucks, right? *Wrong*. Straight after registration Miss Rossiter goes, 'Now, who can tell me something about the Second World War?'

My hand goes up like a rocket.

'Yes, Georgie?'

'Miss, it was us and the Germans. It started in nineteen thirty-nine, ended in nineteen forty-five. We won.'

'Excellent, Georgie, though it wasn't just us and the Germans, you know. Anyway.' She rubs her hands together briskly and smiles round the class. 'Starting today, we're going to find out all about the Home Front in the Second World War.'

'Hey, *cool!*' I can't help it, it just comes out.

She freezes me with ice-blue eyes. 'There's nothing cool about it, Georgie, but it *is* very interesting, because the Home Front means ordinary people like you and me. Some of your grandmas and grandads were children at the time: you could begin by asking them what they remember about it. They might even have a few mementoes hidden away: snapshots, ration books, a gas mask – that sort of thing. If so, perhaps they'll let us borrow them so we can have a display table.'

'Miss?' My hand's up again.

'What is it, Georgie?'

'Miss, I went to Eden Camp Saturday with my mum and dad. It was great.'

'What *is* Eden Camp, Georgie?'

'It's this World War Two museum, miss, in an old prison camp. There's—'

'Just a minute.' She stops me. 'Why don't you come out here and tell us all about it, Georgie? It'll be the perfect lift-off for our topic.'

So I stand out front and tell 'em all about the place. The twenty-nine huts and what's in 'em. Well, most of them. The Hurricane and the doodlebug. It's good when I mention the doodlebug because Miss Rossiter stops me and asks me what a doodlebug was and you can tell she doesn't know herself. So here's Professor Wetherall delivering his famous lecture on the doodlebug, also known as the V-1 or the buzz-bomb. I really lay it on. Timothy Wright keeps mouthing 'Creep' and 'Swot' at me behind his hand so the teacher won't see. He's a face on him like a slapped bum 'cause *he's* usually the one who gets to show off.

It takes me till break to get through everything because Miss Rossiter keeps asking questions. I can answer 'em all as well, and when the buzzer sounds she goes, 'That was *fascinating*, Georgie, thank you.' She turns to the class. 'Wasn't it fascinating, everybody?'

A few kids nod and growl yes, but I can feel them hating me. When I get outside a bunch of the guys're waiting. They get me down, rub chewing-gum in my hair and write SWOT across my forehead with a felt-tip. I spend the whole break scrubbing it off and I look like a second-hand bog-brush when I walk into the next lesson.

Two minutes later I'm a *hero* bog-brush, because Miss Rossiter's spent her break talking to old Hollings about Eden Camp and he's given her the green light to organise a class trip. Wendy Slingsby dives in her bag and passes me a spray-can of something that dries up chewing-gum, and Elizabeth Morton lends me this folding brush with a mirror in the handle.

Suddenly I'm flavour of the month, and handsome with it.

Six

Doesn't last. Never does, have you noticed? The second I walk in the door Mum goes, 'Oh so *there* you are: don't take your blazer off, you're going straight out again.'

'Huh? Where'm I *going*, Mum?'

'Across to Miss Coverley's.'

'Oh no: I'm not asking *her* about the Blitz, she hates me. I'll look it up on the Internet.'

'You're not going about the *Blitz*, Georgie, unless you mean the Blitz you inflicted on the poor lady's dahlias yesterday.'

'Dahlias? *What* dahlias? What you *on* about, Mum?'

'You know exactly what I'm on about, young man. You've been dashing across people's gardens again, you and those two delinquents you knock about with. You barged straight across Miss Coverley's flowerbed, trampled her dahlias flat and damaged her fence getting away. And don't bother to deny it: she came knocking on my door at ten this morning, really upset.'

'I told you, Mum: she *hates* me. I see her gawping at me through her window every time I pass. She's exaggerating to get me in trouble.'

'Don't be *stupid*, Georgie. Miss Coverley's a sweet old lady. Why on earth would she hate you? What she hates is having her garden wrecked when she's spent hours and hours making it nice, and I don't blame her, so I'll tell you what you're going to do. You're going to walk over there right now, knock on her door and apologise.'

'Aw, *Mu*-um!'

'Never mind *Aw Mum*. I've paid for the damage you caused with five pounds, and that will be deducted from your pocket money on Saturday. You won't need money on Saturday anyway, because you'll be busy repairing the fence you damaged.'

''S not *fair*: it wasn't just me. What about Pete and Danny? *They* broke the fence down too.'

'Well, Georgie, if you can persuade Peter and Daniel to work *with* you on Saturday, I'm sure Miss Coverley won't object, but mending fences isn't as much fun as knocking them down and I fancy you'll find your friends have other things to do.'

I know, I know. You're thinking, *I wouldn't do it, I'd tell her to go take a running jump. I'd tell* both *of 'em to take a running jump*, but you see, you don't know my dad. If I told Mum to take a running jump he'd rip my head off and pour boiling oil down the inside of my neck, and if you don't believe me *you* can take a running jump.

Seven

So I goes across to Miss Coverley's feeling puky all the way. I can hardly make my feet keep going in the right direction. I'm like, *It's no use: I can't do this, I just can't.* I decide to walk off instead, down town or somewhere: I can say I apologised, then went for a walk. I'm telling myself this and all the time I know it's a non-starter, because Mum'll have told the old bag to expect me. If I don't show up she'll grass and Dad'll get involved.

Don't you just hate it when you're trapped?

I knock softly, hoping she won't hear. A lot of old people're deaf, right? Not her though. She must've been waiting behind the door because it opens straight away and there she is, gawping at me as usual.

'Oh, Miss Coverley.' I try to sound sincere. 'I guess I owe you an apology.'

'I believe you do, young man.' She's gazing into my eyes like she's trying to hypnotise me or something. Weird.

'Seems me and my mates accidentally dámaged some flowers when we took a shortcut across your garden yesterday. We didn't mean to and I'm sorry.'

'Hmmm.' She compresses her purply lips. 'Shortcut my eye: creeping, I believe it's called, and it's got to stop.'

'I've apologised, paid for the damage.'

'To my dahlias, not the fence. I want the fence repaired.'

I nod. 'Mum told me. I'll come Saturday.'

'I accept your apology. When I was your age there was no such thing as creeping: lads wouldn't have dared. There's no respect these days, no consideration. I'll see you on Saturday then.'

'Yes.' I start to turn away, stop myself. 'Can I ask you something, Miss Coverley?'

'What?'

'I don't mean to sound cheeky, but sometimes I notice you looking at me. Mum says I'm being stupid but . . .'

She nods. 'You remind me of somebody. Somebody I knew a long time ago. Don't worry about it.'

'Thanks for telling me. And no, I won't worry.'

I go home for my tea, glad to have the embarrassing ordeal behind me. I get some earache from Dad when he comes in but I'm not fussed. I've had the satisfaction of telling Mum I'm right, old Coverley *has* been gawping at me.

I don't know it, but something's lying in wait up ahead that'll make all this stuff seem like nothing.

Eight

Tuesday morning I gets Pete and Danny together in the yard and I'm like, 'Guess what I've got lined up for Saturday, fellas.'

'Haven't got a clue,' goes Danny, 'but I bet it's got something to do with World War Two.'

'Nope.'

'Must be spending it in bed, then,' quips Pete.

'You're a devil-may-care jokester, Peter,' I tell him.

'So go on then,' says Danny, 'what *have* you got lined up?'

'I'm only fixing old Coverley's fence, aren't I: the one you two helped to flatten Sunday.'

'*No*,' goes Pete. 'What you want to do *that* for, Georgie?'

Danny shakes his head. 'He's flipped, Pete. Must have. Or else he's joined the scouts and this'll be his good deed for the day.'

'Hah-ha-ha.' I laugh, then switch to my mean look. 'No, I haven't flipped *or* joined the scouts. The old bag grassed me up to my folks. My mum gave her five pounds out of my pocket money, told her I'd mend her rotten fence and sent me across to apologise. It was the worst minute of my life.'

'I wouldn't have done it,' says Pete straight away.

'I knew you'd say that. I was waiting for it.'

'*I* wouldn't either,' goes Danny. 'I'd rather stick needles in my eyes.'

I shake my head. 'You'd have done it if you had *my* dad. Anyway, that's not the point. The point is, we all did it and I'm stuck with putting it right, so I hope you'll come and help.'

'Saturday, did you say?' goes Pete.

'Yeah.'

He pulls a face. 'Sorry, mate, I've promised to mind my little sister Saturday while Mum and Dad go to the garden centre. If it'd been *Sunday* . . .'

'Well it's *not*,' I snap. 'What about you, Danny?'

He shakes his head. 'You're not going to believe this, Georgie . . .'

'Probably not.' *Mum was right, then.*

'We're off to my gran's at Yarcombe. It's been arranged ages, honestly.' He shrugs. 'I'd do *anything* to get out of it, but you know how families are.'

'Sure.' I gaze at them. 'And now I know how *mates* are. Catch you later, when I'm not looking for help.'

'Hey, just a minute . . .'

'Don't be like *that*, Georgie . . .'

I don't look back.

Nine

I keep it up all week. Avoid them at break. Hang back at hometime till they've gone. Leave my mobile switched off. They're really fussed, you can tell. Serve 'em right.

Tuesday we all get letters to take home about the trip to Eden Camp, which Rossiter has fixed for Thursday week. Parents have to sign and send the dosh. I'm chuffed 'cause it makes it seem close.

Nothing else happens. Friday Pete and Danny wait in the yard till nearly four. I'm in the PE store, watching through the window. You should've seen 'em pacing up and down, muttering, looking at the door. They're probably ready to apologise, but with the job still in front of me I'm not ready to let 'em.

Don't parents *suck*? I get home to find mine have arranged a trip Saturday to Alton Towers for themselves and Emily. We *never* go out two Saturdays in a row: they've done it so I miss out on something good while I'm fixing Coverley's fence. Extra punishment. When Dad tells me I lose it a bit: shout that it's unfair, which it is, but him and Mum just laugh and call me Kevin, after the character on TV. I can't stand it when they do that, like *they* were never young.

Anyway I'm damned if I'm going to moon around while they load the car, so next morning at eight I'm knocking on the old bag's door in my tattiest kit, with Dad's sledge-hammer and toolbox under my arm. I'm hoping she's still in bed so she has to come stumbling down half-asleep in curlers and some sad old nightie, but she's up. Been up for hours, most likely. She takes me round the back and shows me how she wants it done, and two doors up the Sanderson land-shark hears and starts barking like crazy. Maybe old Sanderson'll bring it round: encourage it to pull lumps off me while I work.

Turns out we broke a post, so my first job is to dig out the stump. It's rotten, of course, which is why it couldn't even support three skinny kids. It'd have fallen over by itself about an hour later, but there you go. I get the thing out and stand the new post, which Coverley's had delivered from somewhere during the week, in the hole. What with the barking and the thump of my sledge-hammer, I don't hear the departure of my loving family. I hope a tyre blows out on a lonely road in a cloudburst.

There's no sign of Pete or Danny, by the way. They *might* be as sorry as they looked in the yard yesterday, but it hasn't made 'em break any arrangements like they broke this fence.

The post's the only new bit. I have to pull out some bent, rusty staples to free the fence-panel from the broken post, then secure it to the new post with staples out of Dad's box. Doesn't take long to tell, but the whole job occupies two and a half hours and I'm sweating like a pig 'cause it's hot. If the old trout was paying me the national minimum wage I'd have about ten quid to draw, but I'm paying *her*. I try rocking the fence and it's dead firm, and as I stand back and look at it I get a good feeling, which surprises me. She must've been spying, because the glass door slides open and she comes shuffling out with a steaming mug in her knobbly fist.

'Here, you must be ready for a nice drop of char.' I nod, smile, take the mug. She grips the new post, tries moving it. 'Hmmm. Nice job, Georgie.'

I feel her watching me as I sip the tea. *Wonder who it is I remind her of? Old boyfriend, maybe.* The idea that some guy might once have fancied old Coverley seems so far-fetched I can't get my head round it so I give it up, nod at the fence. 'Last a while, I reckon.'

'It'll last till some young hooligan decides to use these gardens as an assault course,' she says, then looks at me. 'Won't be you though, Georgie. Not now. We feel different about things we've built ourselves. Tell your mates to lay off, and it'll be fine. More char?'

'No. No more, thanks. This was plenty.' I hand back the mug. 'If everything's OK I think I'll get back.'

She nods. 'Everything's OK, Georgie, thank you. We'll be seeing each other around.'

'Yes.' It's obvious she doesn't hate me, and I find I quite like her. I load myself with tools, nod and walk off. I've no idea why, but I'm *glad* I spent the morning fixing the fence instead of going to Alton Towers.

Ten

Sunday I phone Pete at seven a.m. for the hell of it. 'Job's done,' I bellow. 'I forgive you.' He's a zombie, no idea who's calling, what it's about. I cut him off.

The sun's hot already, so after breakfast I put on racing shades and boogie along to Sparrow Park. There's nobody about, but I'm confident Pete will work out who called and tell Danny and they'll show up in due course. Meanwhile I'm a British agent in Hitler's Berlin waiting to rendezvous with my contact, Gunther. I sit looking nonchalant as Gestapo operatives disguised as dog-walkers come and go, oblivious to the fact that the wimpy-looking guy on the bench is the legendary Shadow, a master of espionage with a price on his head.

My so-called mates approach around half nine. I pretend not to see them.

'Got the message, Georgie!' warbles Pete. 'You get earlier and earlier.'

'Yeah,' goes Danny, 'he was on to *me* before eight.'

'That right?' I'm still the Shadow; they can't see where I'm looking.

'That's right: ten to, to be exact. Anyway, here we are.'

'Weren't here yesterday though, were you?' I'm looking past him.

'I *explained* about that, Georgie: I had to go to my gran's at—'

'Yarcombe,' I supply, flatly.

'Yeah, and *I* was looking—'

'After your little sister, I know.' *Squirm, you rats.*

'Look, mate . . .'

I shake my head. 'No, *you* look. It was hot, like today. I'd to swing a sledge-hammer with one hand while holding a post with the other. Could've used a little help, know what I'm saying? As it was I sweated, pulled a muscle, cut myself. Look.' I showed them. 'We all *broke* that fence but I was the only one mending it. I woke up this morning with a headache, which is what the shades're for. So if you guys want me around you better treat me right, OK?'

It's really good. I don't miss the fiver Mum gave Coverley because they shell out for everything at Wendy's and I'm not just talking drinks. After that I reckon they've suffered enough and lighten up, and by dusk we're mates just like before. If I'd known how desperately I'd soon be missing those two loons, I wouldn't have put 'em through it in the first place.

Eleven

We start our display table. I kick it off Monday with two of my models: the Matilda tank and the Stuka. Miss Rossiter threatens my street cred again by cooing over them, saying she hadn't realised I was so talented. Timothy Wright pretends to puke on the floor when she isn't looking. Everybody's forgotten to ask around for stuff, but my contribution reminds them and on Tuesday Eve Eden arrives with a ration book, a silver ARP badge and her grandma's Mickey Mouse gas mask. She's a big-head, Eve Eden: reckons Eden Camp was named after her grandad. I say, 'Yeah, and I suppose Witchfield's named after your mum, 'cause she's a witch.'

It seems like for ever till Thursday, but it finally rolls round. Turns out to be one of those misty mornings when there's dew on the spider webs but you can feel the sun starting to burn through. I say 'bye to Mum same as always and walk off into the haze, with no notion of what I'll have to go through before I see her again.

The coach is parked in the yard. We have register, then line up in the hall for the usual lecture from the head, old Hollings. 'Remember,' he goes, 'when you are out there, each one of you is an ambassador. Tell us what an *ambassador* does, Ian Pickersgill.'

'Sir, he fights bulls.'

'*No*, lad, you're thinking of a *matador*. Tell him, Eve Eden.'

'Sir, he's a representative. He represents his country, usually abroad. Some ambassadors are women.'

'Thank you, Eve. Did you get that, Ian Pickersgill?'

'Yes, sir.'

'Splendid.' He smiles. 'Today, you are all ambassadors for Witchfield Middle School. You will be seen by a lot of people, and the impression you make on them is the impression they will form of our school. If you screech and yell, push and shove, pick your nose in the lunch queue and shy Cornish pasties at one another, they're not going to think much of Witchfield Middle School. *Are* they, Silas Warner?'

'No, sir.'

'No, sir. If, on the other hand, you move quietly from place to place, conversing in low tones, listening for your teacher's instructions and complying with them, then people will be impressed. *Witchfield Middle is obviously a fine school*, they'll say, and that's the sort of thing we all *want* them to say, isn't it, Barry Naylor?'

'Yes, sir.'

'Good.' He smiles again, rubs his hands together. 'Off you go then: have a lovely time, and try to learn something you never knew before. Lead off, Miss Rossiter.'

Good job it's not raining: flipping coach could rust *away*, the way he blathers on.

Twelve

If you're one of those people who only believe what they see, you might as well stop at this point. What follows is every bit as true as what's gone before, but now it gets weird.

Still with me? *Your* funeral then.

As we swing into the car park it feels like coming home. To me, I mean. None of the others have been here before. I'm pumped up, ready to show off big-time. It isn't every day you know more about a subject than your teacher, and I've an idea Miss Rossiter's going to use me as a resource here. I've even swotted up a bit on the rise of Hitler, which is what hut 1 is about.

She doesn't ask me anything in hut 1 but I'm not bothered: there are twenty-nine huts, plenty of time. We spend ages in hut 2 because it's about the Home Front, which is our topic at school. I drop the word 'spiv', and Miss Rossiter has me tell everybody what that was, so that's good.

Hut 3's about U-boats. U-boats were German submarines. 'Of course, U-boat stands for *Unterseeboot*,' I say casually. 'Everyone knows that.' Teacher doesn't though: I'm in my element.

The theme of hut 4 is 'Britain Prepares'. It's got some stuff about gas masks, so of course big-head Eve Eden has to start on about her grandma's Mickey Mouse gas mask. You should've heard her: you'd think her grandma flipping *invented* the gas mask, the way she goes on. We're in there ten minutes and I don't get a word in edgeways.

Hut 5's next though: my favourite. I'll make sure everybody hears me in there, no danger. There'll be sirens and bombs and ack-ack guns and fire bells, but all that'll be *nothing* compared to Eve Eden yapping.

As it turns out, hut 5's as far as I'm going to get. *Try to learn something you didn't know before*, old Hollings said, and I'm about to. By golly I am.

Thirteen

There's this house in hut 5: a bombed-out London house with glass and bricks and smashed furniture. I think I mentioned it before. It's dark, and you hear planes and guns and fire bells. It's dead realistic. All the kids love it – I knew they would. They're hanging over the barrier and I'm pointing stuff out to them. The burst water pipe, the leaning wall, a kid's hand poking up out of the rubble. I can't really tell you what happens then: I must be overexcited or something because one second I'm with the others and the next I'm scrambling up that drift of broken bricks towards the dummy hand, pretending I'm a rescuer. I know it's stupid but I can't help myself, even when I hear Miss Rossiter bark. I suppose in a minute or two some guy would've come running to haul me out of there, but then I feel a scary lurch like the brick pile's starting to slide and Eden Camp's gone. It's still dark and the noises're the same but it's cold, there's no barrier and the hand in the rubble is real.

Fourteen

I know what's happened to me, that's the worst part. You've read 'em, and if you haven't you've seen them on TV. I'm talking about time-slip stories, where some kid goes through a certain door or picks up a particular object and finds himself back in the eighteenth century or the stone age or some other time. There's loads of books like that, and videos, but none of 'em touch the horror. I mean, a kid lands somewhere back in the past and *bang*, he's straight into the action: dodging the tyrannosaur or the highwayman or whatever baddie he finds himself up against. He's never shown the way he'd really be: paralysed with shock, not because there's a dinosaur or a bunch of cut-throats, but because his mum and dad aren't born yet. You don't need dinosaurs or cut-throats or a little kid buried under rubble to make it scary: all you need is a second to work out what's happened, and a minute to start to realise what it means.

I'd love to claim I try to save the kid but I don't. I don't. What I do is slip and slide down that brick pile, howling for my mum. What I do is set off running along a black, smashed-up street looking through tear-blurred eyes for the barrier, the coach, Eve Eden. I'm insane, I suppose. Temporarily insane. I'm looking for something – *anything* – familiar, yet I know I won't find it because it isn't here, isn't *yet*. I don't know how far I run. It must be pretty far because I end up shattered and out of breath. I've seen people. Not many, but one of them might be Miss Rossiter or someone from Eden Camp so I go up close to look. They all turn out to be strangers with troubles of their own. No one's interested in a frightened boy. After a bit I'm passing a row of shops and deep doorways. I stumble into one and sit down in a corner to get my breath back. I've stopped crying. I wipe my face with my sleeve and stare out at the bit of street I can see. A bell's ringing a long way off, and when a series of flat bangs make the concrete floor vibrate I know I'm hearing bombs: real ones. I don't feel excited or even frightened. In fact I'm not feeling anything much, except cold. Thinking about it now I reckon my mind had gone onto standby mode to keep from burning out. There are some things our brains aren't designed to cope with. Death's one: our *own* death, I mean. The size of the universe is another, and the thought of how tiny and helpless and *unimportant* we are in it. We avoid thinking about these things because instinct tells us they'll drive us mad, and the knowledge that I'm somehow alive before my parents is unmanageable like that.

So I'm on standby mode, the empty street's my screen saver and if I sit absolutely still, maybe I'll make it to morning.

Fifteen

Morning. It starts in the pitch dark but I know it's morning because people're passing: the odd one at first then more and more, some on pushbikes, most on foot. I guess they're on their way to work. I keep still so nobody'll notice me.

By my watch it's half five, but I don't know whether that means anything. After all it's summer back in Witchfield, autumn here. If the *season*'s different, why should the time be the same?

My bum's numb. I'm stiff, cold and hungry. My summer uniform of blazer, shirt and trousers is totally inadequate, but none of these things is uppermost in my mind because I'm scared. Really, *really* scared. Not of bombs. The bangs stopped hours ago and anyway I'm not even thinking about bombs. I'm scared of what will happen when I approach somebody and start telling them how I come to be here: a policeman, say. I know I'll have to ask for help eventually if I'm not to freeze or starve, but if I say I've come from 2002 he'll probably cart me off to the loony-bin. Couldn't blame him, right? And if I tell him something else: that I've run away, hitched a hundred miles from Witchfield, he'll want to get me home. *What's your address?* he'll say, and *Do your folks know where you are?* and when I tell him my address won't *exist* till 1969 and my folks aren't born yet I'll be in that rubber room so fast my feet won't touch. I bet you're smiling, but there's nothing funny about it at the time.

Anyway, I have to move in the end 'cause I'm busting to pee. It's still dark, so I wait till nobody's passing and dodge into the next doorway. I know it isn't very nice to pee in the doorway of somebody's shop, but what else can I do in the circumstances? Once on my feet I don't fancy getting down on the concrete again so I start walking along the street, shoulders hunched against the cold. Walking cures the numbness and warms my feet a bit but I'm still freezing. There are quite a few people about, but I avoid eye contact and nobody speaks to me.

After a minute or two I see a wide gateway straight ahead and a building that looks like some sort of factory. Everybody's going through the gateway with PEEK FREAN over it. I recognise the name; they do biscuits. There's a foody smell in the air which makes my guts yearn and my mouth water. As I come closer I see that there's a mobile canteen just outside the gates and three or four people with steaming mugs. I'd been about to change course and hurry past the factory, but hunger makes me brave. I fish in my pocket for change, approach the counter.

'Yes, mate?'

'Tea, please, and do you do burgers?' I keep my voice low to avoid drawing attention to myself.

'You *what*?' Big red-faced guy, voice like a foghorn.

'I'd like some tea, and if you don't do burgers a ham sandwich.'

'A ham sandwich? *Ham?*' He laughs wheezily, shaking his head. 'Where've *you* been, mate? Don't you know there's a war on?' The tea drinkers're looking at me.

''Course I do,' I say. 'Cheese, then.'

'Tea, cheese sarnie.' He turns away to get it, clucking and shaking his head. I stare at the ground, praying nobody'll speak to me. I'm practically falling over with hunger.

'Hey, tosh, what's a burger?'

I turn. The speaker's a thin lad of about fifteen, queuing behind me. I shrug. 'Burger, you know: *hamburger*?'

'You an American, then?'

'No.'

'Where you from, then?'

'I'm English.'

'Don't sound English.' He looks at the knot of drinkers. 'Don't *sound* English, does he?'

'Leave 'im be, Alfie,' growls a fat woman. 'He's just a kid.'

''Ere y'are.' The foghorn slides a plate and mug across the counter. 'Fourpence.'

'Four.' I don't have it exact, give him a twenty.

''Ere, what's *your* little game, sunshine? What the heck's *this*?'

It hits me like a kick in the stomach: *Of course – my dosh is useless here.* He wraps a brawny forearm round my breakfast, throws the twenty on the cobbles. Everybody's staring at me. 'Gerraarofit!' he roars. 'Go *On*, before I call a copper.'

They're all laughing. Those who care about me are unreachably far away, I'm facing death from hypothermia and starvation and all these guys do is laugh. I turn and run.

Sixteen

I cross a main road and find myself in a park. It's just getting light. Running has warmed me up a bit but I'm light-headed from hunger. Thirsty too. I walk along a tree-lined pathway hoping to find a drinking fountain, but I only find a bandstand and some benches. I can't walk any further. I sit down on a bench, wrap my arms round my body and rock, gazing at the bandstand. I start thinking about the sunny bench in Sparrow Park and my two mates Pete and Danny, and our house just a short walk down Cardigan Road, my mum doing me bacon and sausages and my nice warm bed upstairs. I get an aching lump in my throat. Another second and I'll burst out crying, but then I hear a motor and a van appears, moving slowly under the bare trees. It's olive drab like an army vehicle, and as it draws level I see it has an open hatch like the mobile canteen from outside the biscuit factory, with a narrow counter. In the dark behind the counter I think I see a woman.

The van passes the bandstand and turns off down a narrow path. I follow it with my eyes, convinced it carries food. It passes from sight. Seconds later the growl of its motor is drowned by what sounds like guys cheering. I get up, walk across to the narrow path and follow it, and that's how I find the searchlight battery.

As soon as I see it I know what it is. A horseshoe-shaped wall of sandbags surrounds a fat concrete pillar in the middle of a grassy area. The massive light sits tilted on top of the pillar, its lens reflecting the dawn. The van has parked and the searchlight crew is jostling round the hatch.

I hide behind a tree. There are five guys with tin mugs. As a man reaches the front of the queue he passes his mug up to the woman, who fills it from an urn I can't see and hands it back steaming, together with a sandwich. Once served the men lean against the sandbags, sipping and chewing. Saliva fills my mouth as I watch, and my stomach growls. I'm gathering courage to show myself when the last man leaves the hatch and the van lurches off across the grass, followed by another cheer from the crew.

I can't stand it a second longer. As the vehicle disappears I leave my hiding-place and approach the men, resolved to beg if I must.

A short, red-headed guy spots me first. 'Hello,' he cries, 'where'd *you* spring from, son?'

'I was passing. Please . . .' I stare at his half-eaten sandwich. 'I'm *very* hungry, haven't eaten since . . .'

'Oh . . . oh right, here y'are son.' He tears the sandwich in two, hands one piece to me. I cram it into my mouth, nod my thanks. They all watch me chew. Normally I'd be embarrassed but as it is I'm too hungry to care.

A guy with a stripe on his sleeve offers his cheese roll untouched. I take it and he says, 'Shame you didn't show up half a minute sooner, lad: ladies'd have seen you all right.'

'Who *are* they?' I manage, between mouthfuls.

'WVS. Save our ruddy lives, don't they, lads?'

Murmurs of assent. Redhead passes his mug. 'Here: wet your whistle. Bit early for school, aren't you?'

'I don't go to school.'

'What's the rig, then?' He means my uniform.

'I mean, my school's not round here.'

'Ah.' He grins knowingly. 'Runaway, eh? Evacuation billet didn't suit, that it?'

I shake my head, thankful I know some stuff about the war. 'I'm not an evacuee. I . . . lost my parents.'

'Oh.' He looks uncomfortable. They all do. 'That's . . . that's terrible, son. Who looks after you?'

I feel rotten, like I've taken the guy's grub then lied to him. 'I don't mean they're *dead*: we got sort of separated.' *By sixty-odd years.*

'Ah.' He nods. 'There are places, you know: rest centres where they sort out problems like yours. The bombing's scattered lots of families. If I were you—'

'Yeah, thanks, but I can't. I've got to get back, see? Find where I lost them, and . . .' My voice tails off. I can't say what I'll do then because I don't know myself. I only decided about five seconds ago that the thing to do was return to the spot where the time-slip happened. *Should never have left it in the first place.* I can't turn myself in at some rest centre: not with the story I've got to tell. Time to go.

'Thanks,' I say, 'for the grub, the tea. I'll be OK now. Y'know, they made . . . I mean they'll make a movie about you guys one day.' I don't know why I say this. It sounds stupid and they laugh like the people at the factory. Can't blame them, but I wanted to leave 'em with something nice, that's all, and there *is* a movie. *Light Up the Sky*, it's called. Anyway, while they're laughing I walk away, telling myself I'll need to watch my mouth in future.

Or do I mean in *past*?

Seventeen

I'm on a wide road with two sets of shiny metal rails. *Tramlines*, I tell myself. I've never seen a tram, except on archive footage. I hope one'll come by. It's fully daylight now and it's amazing how optimistic a cheese roll and a few gulps of tea can make you feel. *All I have to do*, I tell myself, *is find that bombed-out house and climb the rubble*. I haven't forgotten the arm, but I think they'll have dug the kid out by now.

The street I'm on is Jamaica Road. There are hundreds of pedestrians but nobody looks at me twice, which is good. I've passed a couple of tram stops and noticed that nobody's waiting, and further up I find out why. There's a gaping hole in the middle of the road. A bomb's torn up the tramlines. They protrude, buckled, over the crater. Two men are fencing it off. I seem to be the only one who's interested. I look away.

I've a pretty good sense of direction, and I reckon if I hang a left about now I'll be pretty close to the street with the bombed-out house. I've crossed one but it was too wide. There's another ahead which feels about right.

Cherry Garden Street it's called, though there isn't a garden in sight. It's like Pleasant Street in Witchfield, which is easily the least pleasant street in town. Whoever dreams up street names has a twisted sense of humour.

Cherry Garden Street turns out to be quite short. It has no cherries and no bombed-out house. I return to Jamaica Road and walk on to the next left, Drummond Road. This looks familiar too, and some houses have been flattened but they're in rows. Mine was by itself. The optimism's flagging a bit.

Trouble is, all the streets look like the one I want. Some have been bombed, some not. They're long, drab and hard on the feet. Mid-morning I'm so desperate I decide to ask someone. A woman's on her hands and knees scrubbing her doorstep, which is comical considering half the street's rubble. 'Excuse me?'

'Whatcha want, dear?'

'I'm looking for a house that was hit last night, caved in on a little kid.'

'Shame. What street?'

'I dunno.'

'You don't *know*?' She peers at me. 'Shouldn't you be at school, son?'

'They closed it. I just need to find—'

'Where's your gas mask? Not supposed to be out without your gas mask, y'know.'

'It's at home, I forgot it.'

She narrows her eyes. 'Where's *home*, son? Not from around here, are you?'

'No. That's why I've got to find the house, see, so I can get back.' I nod towards her glistening doorstep. 'I'll let you get on. Sorry to bother you.'

'*Oi*, not so fast.' She's getting to her feet. 'You're *lost*, entcha? I think I better take you up Christ Church Centre. There's people there who'll . . .'

I'm gone.

Eighteen

'Are you looking for somebody, dear?'

'No. There was a boy just now in Lockwood Road I think's lost. Reckon he's looking for a house where a little kid was killed last night. Something not quite right about him, thought I best tell someone.'

'I see. Well, Mrs . . .?'

'Staples. Edna Staples, eleven Lockwood Road.'

'Well, Mrs Staples, I understand your concern, but you see this is a rest centre. If you can persuade the boy to come in, we'll do all we can to help him, but I'm afraid it's not part of our function to go out onto the streets looking for lost children. Apart from anything else, we haven't got the staff.'

'No, but I thought . . .'

'I'm sorry, but you know what it's been like these past few days: chaos. It's all very well the papers saying we can take it: they're not up at the sharp end, they don't see the shattered lives. There are probably a hundred youngsters wandering about out there: orphans, runaway evacuees and so forth. If we were to go out and try to round them all up, there'd be nobody left to run the centre. You could try the police, but I fancy they've got their work cut out, what with the blackout, looters, fifth-columnists and I don't know what.'

'I ain't going to the police. I just thought . . . still, never mind. Have to shift for himself, I suppose; poor little blighter.'

Nineteen

I wander about, but without the street name I've no chance. I might have passed it already and not recognised it. My brain's getting clogged up with other stuff, I'm not concentrating. I'm fussed about having no gas mask, which wouldn't have occurred to me if that woman hadn't mentioned it. Daylight's fading and I dread another night on the street in my summer clothes. I'm hungry again. I'm even wondering what day it is, what *month*. You wouldn't believe how disoriented you feel when you don't know stuff like that. In the end I spot a discarded newspaper on a bench, pick it up and look at the date: 4 October 1940. It's a Friday, same as it'll be at home in 2002. Makes me feel better, don't ask me why. I notice a clock above a jeweller's shop and set my watch by it. *Right*, I tell myself, *now I know what everybody else knows.*

I know what everybody else knows and a lot only *I* know. I know when this war ends, for a start, and who wins. I'm probably the only guy in London who isn't fretting about invasion. Mind you, I've plenty to fret about without that. Still. I could go into a betting shop and put dosh on the exact date the war will end and I'd probably get odds of 10,000 to 1. I'd be rolling in it. Two snags: my dosh is useless and there's no such thing as a betting shop in 1940.

Then *this* comes into my head: *my grandad's four*. I'm the only kid in the world with a four-year-old grandad. If this was Witchfield instead of London I could take my grandad for a ride in his pushchair, for Pete's sake. Oh: in case you're wondering,

I know I'm in London because I've seen tube stations and loads of other clues. I'm not daft, though it's a wonder the fix I'm in hasn't driven me round the bend.

Dangerous knowledge. Yes, I really *will* have to watch my mouth. I've read enough about the war to know that in 1940 everybody's paranoid about spies. German spies, and also fifth-columnists: Brits who are secretly working for the enemy. I've read about Polish airmen being arrested because of their accent, and people getting shot by the Home Guard because they happen to loiter near an aircraft factory. I've only to let something slip – something that doesn't quite fit – and I could be in deep trouble. Think about it: guy without ID or ration book, no birth certificate, clothes cut in funny styles from uninvented fabrics, vocabulary strewn with unfamiliar words; no home, parents, school, friends, aunties or uncles: a kid from nowhere in fact. They'll lock me up for life, or shoot me.

It's six o'clock. Nearly dark. I've just turned onto Keetons Road when the sirens wail and people start hurrying in all directions – I guess towards shelters. I've no idea where to go. I can't afford to get shut in some shelter with people who might start asking me stuff. I break into a jog so I look like everybody else, but a minute later there *isn't* anybody else: just Georgie Wetherall, the Boy from the Future, jogging along a pitch-black empty road to the sirens' shivery yodel.

'*Oi!*' I skid to a halt in time to avoid colliding with a bulky guy I haven't seen in the blackout. He's wearing a tin hat. 'Where the thundering heck d'you think *you're* going – can't you hear the siren?' He's a silver badge in his lapel like the one Eve Eden brought to school. *Will bring to school.*

I nod. 'Yes, but I don't know where to go.'

'Where d'you *live*?'

'Er . . . Jamaica Road.'

'Too far.' He grabs my arm. 'Come on.' He starts hurrying me along, muttering under his breath. The siren stops and I hear planes like at Eden Camp. A building looms: long, low place, no windows. '*Get* in there, don't budge till the all-clear.' He shoves me at a doorway with a curtain that feels like sacking. I stumble through, trip over somebody's legs, dive onto a mattress of soft flesh.

'Oooh!' Woman in pain. 'Rupture my ruddy *spleen*, why don'tcha?'

'Sorry.'

'*Sorry?* I'll give you sorry, you clumsy young bleater. Just you wait till the all-clear.'

'Who *is* it, Doris?' Second woman. Place is packed: can't see anything but there's a fug and it stinks.

'How the ruddy heck should *I* know? Some snotty-nosed little whipper-snapper by the sound of him. *Sorry*. He *will* be, six tomorrow morning.'

'Leave him be, you two.' Old guy. 'He's *lost*, entcha, sparra? Lost in the blackout.'

'Y-yes. I was looking for Jamaica Road.'

'Hooo!' Doris. 'Sure you don't mean *Jamaica*, dearie? Not from round *here*, anyway.'

'No, I'm from Witchfield.'

'*Which*field?' Joker in the dark.

'Witchfield. W-I-T—'

'*Which*field?' Talk about flogging a joke to death. Titters all round. Flat bangs in the distance, like last night. I give up, wrap my arms round my knees. At least it's warm in here.

Twenty

So we sit in the pitch black, listening to their bombs and our guns. Sometimes you hear the whistle of a falling bomb and sense everybody holding their breath. Then the bang, and somebody'll murmur, 'that was close', or 'that was far'. I'm scared stiff. I know from my reading that these shelters can't withstand a direct hit. In 1940 hundreds of people're blown to bits in street shelters.

Presently there's a lull and somebody calls out. 'How about a bit of light, Gordon?'

'All right.' Voice of authority. 'Check the curtains, somebody.'

The woman I fell on gets up, gropes about a bit. 'Doorway's covered, Gordon.'

'Thanks, Doris. Melvin?'

'All set this end, Gordon.'

'Two lanterns then: Vi's and Vincent's. Smoke if you like.'

Somebody strikes a match. A halo of light appears, grows brighter. I look around but the lantern has left a green blob in front of my eyes. I screw them shut till it fades. When I open them a second lantern's burning. The faint, flickering light plasters shadows on the rough brick walls and I see people crammed all together like sardines in a tin: some sitting, some lying. It reminds me of that famous diagram of a slave-ship, bodies fitted into every inch of space. I feel about as welcome as a shark in a jacuzzi.

A baby's been grizzling but the light seems to soothe it. People start chatting, handing round ciggies, lighting up. Smoke curls, gathers under the concrete roof. I'd love to say something smart-assed about passive smoking but of course I don't. I'm in their space, and anyway the smoke's more fragrant than the stink of unwashed bodies. War in books leaves out the smells.

Three kids at the far end have started a game of Snap. Their shrill cries're getting on my nerves. I wonder how these people stand it, night after night. I notice Doris and her friend looking at me. I close my eyes so they won't talk to me. It doesn't work.

'So where's your place on Jamaica Road?' goes the friend. Her name's Maureen. I pretend not to hear but that doesn't work either. She nudges me with her foot. 'Oi, sunshine: I'm talking to you.'

'Uh?' I do my impression of Pete waking up. 'Hnnnnh . . . wha?'

'I said, where's your place on Jamaica Road?'

'Oh, it's er . . . we're near the park.'

'Ah: Hothfield Place then, eh?'

'Uh: yeah, that's right.'

'No it ain't: Hothfield's nowhere near the park *nor* Jamaica Road. You're one of them runaways, entcha? Where'd they send you: *Rye*?'

I shake my head. 'I'm not a runaway. I'm from Witchfield.'

'Where the ruddy heck's Witchfield? Never heard of it.'

'Near Northampton.'

'Ho, *North-bleat'n-hampton*: and I suppose Mater and Pater brought you hup to London so you wouldn't miss the jolly old *bombing*, what?' She shakes her head. 'Pull the other one, son: it's got bells on it.'

The bombing's started again or I'd get up and leave, stuff the all-clear. As it is it sounds closer than before so I've no choice but to sit tight. I've just decided my only chance is to play dumb when a big one goes off so close it shakes the ground and showers everybody with cement dust. Somebody screams. People stand up, coughing and knocking muck off their clothes with their hands. The baby's howling again. A voice yells, 'For gawd's sake put them ruddy lights out, they can *see* us.' This can't be true with fires burning all over the city but it *feels* true. The lanterns are extinguished. Everybody goes quiet except the baby's mother, who's shushing it desperately as though the flyers might *hear* it. The smoke's invisible now, the blackness sprinkled with the glowing tips of cigarettes.

Twenty-One

Bit by bit I move away from Doris and Maureen, making myself even more unpopular in the process. Sighs and clucks mark my progress as I shuffle on my bottom, nudging recumbent bombees. That's a word I make up to pass the time, by the way: bombee. If the Germans are the bombers, we must be the bombees. Stands to reason.

The night feels endless. If you've ever sat on concrete for twelve hours in the dark you'll know what I mean. My bum feels bruised. There's no room to lie down and sitting hunched makes my spine ache. And I feel so, so lonely. Sounds daft, I know: lonely in the middle of a hundred people; but it's not. They know one another, or at least everybody knows *someone*: I can hear them whispering, chuckling. I know nobody and nobody knows me, and what with that and the knowledge I have but must never divulge, I might as well come from another planet. And when somebody starts singing a song and everybody else joins in I feel so out of it I have a bit of a blub: can't help it. 'Lord and Lady Whatsis' the song's called, and they belt it out so at least nobody hears my sobs.

The bombing keeps up, and the guns. I manage to quit blubbing by the time the singing stops. I think about the guys in the park with their searchlight. *They* know me in a way, but they'll be too busy right now to spare me a thought. Forgotten me altogether, most likely.

Sometime in the early hours, woozy with hunger and fatigue, I have this weird thought: if a bomb gets us it'll mean I'm dead before my parents are even born. Does that mean I never get born and, if so, how come I was at Eden Camp? Does the fact that I'm here mean this shelter *can't* be hit while I'm in it – can't have *been* hit, I mean – on the night of 4 October 1940? Otherwise my folks'll never have me. Or *could* it be hit, and a kid called Georgie Wetherall disappears mysteriously while on a school trip to Eden Camp in 2002? People *do* just vanish: thousands every year in Britain alone, and some are never seen again. Maybe the same thing happens to them that's happened to me: caught in a time-slip and can't get back. Condemned to live in the past and die before they were born.

Do your head in to think about, right?

The all-clear goes at six with dawn light seeping through the sacking. People get up, gather their stuff and shuffle off with bedrolls under their arms to see whether they still have a house, and to go to work or school in the kit they've smoked, sung and slept in. The guy called Gordon's arranging for somebody to take out the two stinking lavatory buckets and empty them, and for somebody else to mop the floor where they've been and re-erect the crude cardboard screen, ready for tonight. Nobody takes any notice of me as I head for the door, and Doris must've forgotten her promise to make me sorry because she isn't waiting outside. I creep off with my shoulders hunched and my hands in my pockets, wondering if I dare try the searchlight crew for a bit of breakfast.

Twenty-Two

A bit later I'm sitting on a low wall, trying to scrape up the energy to walk to the park when I notice something weird. Across the street, on a corner, is a flattened pub. I know it's a pub because there's bits of tables and chairs in the rubble, plus a long green board with a picture of a sailing ship and the words THE VICTORY.

That's not what's weird, though. As I stare across, a movement draws my eye and a kid crawls out from under a table. A boy, seven or eight years old with fair hair, wearing what looks like a cut-down man's suit. He gets up and stands looking back. He hasn't noticed me. Seconds later another kid appears. He's about my age. He's in short trousers and a ragged pullover. A white muffler is wound round his neck. He doesn't see me either. Then a girl pops out wearing a skirt that's about ten sizes too big for her, a fluffy pink cardigan and a navy straw hat with two cherries on it. It's like watching one of those trick TV sequences where thirty-five guys come out of a phone booth. I mean, I'm talking about a *really* small table: just room on top for two glasses and an ashtray. When a fourth kid crawls out I laugh and give myself away.

They swing round, study me for a second or two and cross towards me, looking like kids playing a game of dressing up. I get up. They stop three metres away and the muffler boy says, 'What you laughing at, freckleface?'

Nobody's called me that before. I've got a few freckles, but you'd hardly notice. I nod towards the Victory. 'Didn't half look comical, four of you coming from under that table.'

'Cor, don't he *talk* funny?' goes the girl.

The boy nods, narrows his eyes. 'Yeah, where you *from*, Freckles?'

'Witchfield.'

'Where the heck's that?'

'Northamptonshire.'

'Fancy. What you doing here, then?'

'I . . . ran away.'

'You don't say.' He turns to the others. 'Hear that: Freckles ran away.'

The third boy, a bit older than me, shakes his head. 'Naughty that, very naughty. Don't you know your ma'll be worried about you, Frecks? Worried sick, she'll be.'

I shake my head. 'I didn't run away from my mum, I was evacuated to Witchfield. Couldn't stand the folks I was with.'

The muffler boy eyes me suspiciously. 'You said you *come* from Witchfield, now you say you was *evacuated* there. Which is it, Frecks?'

'Both.' I'm making it up as I go along.

He shakes his head. 'Can't be *both*, Frecks. Know what *I* think?' He's asking his mates, not me.

'What *do* you think, Bertie?' asks the girl.

'I think he's a German spy.'

The older boy nods. 'Could be at that.' He looks at me. 'What's the capital of Scotland, Frecks?'

I want to laugh but I don't. 'Edinburgh.'

'Name the King's two daughters.'

I have to think about this one. They're watching me. After a bit I get it sorted. 'Elizabeth and Margaret.'

'It's *Princess* Elizabeth,' he snarls, 'and *Princess* Margaret. What's the poshest car?'

'Er: Porsche?'

'You *what?*'

'Sounded *German*, Shrapnel,' goes the girl.

I shake my head. 'I said "Posh", that's not German. Rolls-Royce.'

'Right. Who plays the organ on the wireless all the time?'

'Sandy MacPherson.' It's a miracle I know that one: never heard of the guy till I read his name at Eden Camp.

Shrapnel looks at Bertie, shakes his head. 'He's not German.'

Bertie takes over. 'Where you kipping?'

'Nowhere. On the street.'

'Where's your ma, then?'

'Where's *yours?*' I'm getting fed up of this. Bertie's head goes down, he doesn't answer.

'His ma's dead,' says the girl. 'Oil bomb.'

'Oh: sorry, I didn't . . .'

''Course not. Hungry, are you?'

'Bloody right.'

'Oh!' She gasps, looking big-eyed at the others. '"Bloody", he said "bloody".'

I eyeball her. 'You mentioned grub: you got some?'

'Well . . .' She glances at Bertie.

''S all right, Nell.' He looks at me. 'We got grub.' He jerks his head towards the bombed-out pub. 'Over there, only it's top secret, see, and Ma's got to give you the all-clear.'

'I thought your ma . . .'

'Not *my* ma, *Ma*. C'mon.' He sets off back across the road. The others follow him and I follow them. Right then I'd have followed *Hitler* if there'd been a meal in it for me.

Twenty-Three

Under the table is a hole and stone stairs down. I follow the four kids and find myself in what must've been the pub cellar. There are no barrels or bottles, just a sofa and some wooden chairs and tables like those outside, but in better nick. An arched opening in one wall seems to lead to a second cellar. Along another wall stands a stone table with a spirit stove and some pans and cutlery at one end, four Tilley lamps which provide the cellar's only illumination in the middle, and a meat-safe at the other.

I smile 'Nice den. What d'you call yourselves?'

The older boy treats me to a ferocious scowl. 'Wotcha mean, *call* ourselves? Don't call ourselves nuffink.'

'He finks we're a ruddy *gang*,' goes the seven-year-old. 'Don'tcha, Frecks?'

I nod. 'Well, yeah, I assumed so, what with the den and all.'

''T ain't a *den*,' he corrects, 'it's a home. *Our* home. That right, Shrapnel?'

''S right, Mouse. Victory Hall, one of the stately holes of ruddy England.'

'You *live* here?'

'Yeah. Us and a few more. Show him round, Mouse.'

I follow the youngster, making approving noises as he illuminates things with the lamp he's picked up.

'This is where we keeps our cooking fings, and that's what we cooks on, and the grub's in that fing there. Oh, and that's the water tank.' He leads me through the arch into the second cellar. On the floor is a straight row of five mattresses with neatly folded blankets on them. 'We sleep here, 'cept Ma and the girls. They sleep behind that fing.' 'That fing' is a bedspread draped over a clothes-line across one corner. 'That's spare.' He indicates the middle mattress. 'Used to be Spuggy's.'

'What happened to Spuggy?'

The kid shrugs. 'Don't need the bed no more. C'mon.'

There's a trestle table with jugs of water and the basins they wash in, the corner where the 'sweeping fings' are kept, and the chamber-pot. 'The convenience, Ma calls it. She's got 'er own behind the fing.'

'Where's Ma now?' I dare to ask.

'Work, where d'you fink?'

We return to the main cellar. In our absence, Nell's put some broken biscuits and a slim wedge of cheese on a tin plate, which she thrusts at me. ''Ere. 'T ain't much but it's better'n nuffink.' She winks. 'Shrapnel gets the biscuits down Peek Freans.'

I glanced at Shrapnel, who nods. 'Know a geezer, don't I?' He stares at me. 'Top secret, everything here. Right?'

I nod, my mouth crammed with biscuit.

'You don't tell *nobody* what you seen here, what you heard. Blab, and you're out. Bring anybody, or let some geezer foller you, and you're out.'

'You mean . . . you're saying I can *stay* here? Sleep and everything?' I hardly dare hope.

He chuckles. 'Wouldn't've shown you the hole under that chair if you wasn't to stay, Frecks. Mouthful of knuckles, all you'd've seen. Mind . . .' He glances towards the stairs. 'Ma's the gaffer, she gets the final say, but I reckon you'll be all right.'

I could've hugged him.

Twenty-Four

'Who the bleat'n'ell's this, Shrapnel?'

I'm sitting on the sofa peeling spuds when the one they call Ma gets back. I jump up, spilling potatoes onto the floor. She's halfway down the steps, glaring at me, and she's fourteen. If that.

Shrapnel looks sheepish. 'Oh, hello, Ma: this is Frecks. We found him.'

''S all right you *finding* people, Shrapnel: that's the easy part. It's *me*'s got to feed 'em all, keep 'em respectable. How many kites d'you think I can *fill* on fifteen bob a week?'

'It's OK.' I hold up my hands, palms towards her. 'I'll go. The kids were being nice, that's all. It's not a problem, really.' I'm gutted, but they did tell me Ma had the final say.

'Not a problem?' She comes the rest of the way down without taking her eyes off me. 'Got a place then, have you? Fam'ly?'

I shake my head. 'No.'

'So why'd you say it's not a problem?'

'What I mean is, it's not *your* problem. Why should you feed *me* out of your fifteen bob a week? You don't know me from Adam.'

She laughs briefly. Her breath has beer on it. 'I don't know none of *these* urchins from Adam neither, come to that. Look.' She shakes her head. 'Don't mind me: I've had a drop to drink and I'm tired. You can stay.'

'Are you *sure*?' My heart kicks me in the ribs. 'I'll go if you want me to, honestly.'

'I *said* you can stay, er . . . *what* they call you?'

'Frecks. It's short for Freckles, but my *real* name's—'

'Frecks'll do: no real names at Victory Hall. Better see to them spuds, Frecks: I'm famished.'

I gather them up and peel industriously, marvelling at my luck. OK, so I'm still stuck in 1940 but hey: there's grub, a roof, a sort of family. If I'm nice, if I pull my weight here, maybe they'll let me stay till I find that flattened house and go back home.

Twenty-Five

Two more kids show up before the sirens. One, a girl of about twelve, is *called* Siren. The boy is Wotsis, short for Wotsisname. He's elevenish, and his is the only *real* name I learn at Victory Hall. He volunteers it when Ma introduces him to me as Wotsisname. 'Better'n my *real* name,' he mutters; 'better'n bleat'n *Armistead*.'

His pockets bulge with what turn out to be carrots. 'Gorrem for free 'apence, Ma,' he boasts.

Ma eyes him shrewdly. 'Don't come with a bag though, eh? Hope you didn't nick 'em.'

'Would I do a fing like that, Ma?' Eyes like saucers. She doesn't pursue it.

After the sirens, when the bangs've begun, Shrapnel boils up the spuds and carrots on the spirit stove while Ma sits with her feet up. It takes a while, and it doesn't amount to much apiece when he dishes up. It could've done with an onion as well, but I'm not grumbling. Eight people, fifteen bob a week: can't expect burgers and fries even if they'd been invented.

When we've eaten, which doesn't take long, I offer to wash up. Shrapnel's left a panful of water on the stove for the purpose. He produces a chipped enamel bowl from under the table and I pour the warm water into it. 'Any liquid?' I ask.

'What sort of liquid?'

'You know: washing-up liquid.'

'*That's* your washing-up liquid, Frecks.' He points to the water with an expression on his face like he thinks I'm taking the mickey. Too late, I realise I've dropped a clanger. 'Soap, I mean. Soapflakes?'

Ma overhears. 'Don't run to soapflakes, son: don't always have *water*. Leave it to Shrapnel if you can't manage.'

'I can manage, Ma.'

I do. Nell comes and wipes. I say, 'Where does Ma work?' The others've started a sing-song.

'Shop near Tower Bridge. Old geezer sells second-hand clothes. Ma helps out, minds the place when he's down the pub, which is most of the time.' She frowns. 'What did you mean, washing-up liquid?'

I shake my head. 'Slip of the tongue. How does she come to be looking after you and the others?'

Nell shrugs. 'She was evacuated, didn't like where she was, came back to the smoke. Couldn't find her family, wandered about, saw Mouse disappearing down his hole.' She grins. '*This* hole. Place was too big for one and Mouse wasn't looking after hisself too well so she moved in and took him in hand. Then, one by one, the rest of us showed up. She's got a big heart, see? Don't like to fink about kids in doorways. So here we are.'

'And you, Nell: what happened to you?'

'Oh, my dad's in the navy and my mum brought this fella home: Uncle Jim – 'cept he ain't, of course. He's got flat feet so he can't join up: that's what he *says*. He was always coming round and I couldn't stand him so I blew. Ma found me sitting on a bench, crying my eyes out, brought me here. There was only her and Mouse then.'

I don't know what to say after that. We finish washing up, drift across to the sing-song.

There'll be bluebirds over the white cliffs of Dover . . .

I don't actually know it, but I've heard it enough to be able to hum along, and I do. It's not exactly warm in the cellar, but it's a heck of a lot warmer than the street and my stomach's full of spuds and carrots, and I'm as near happy as anybody could be in my predicament.

Twenty-Six

Ma sends Mouse to bed at eight o'clock. His mattress, which he shares with a teddy, is nearest her bedroom. She makes sure he washes his hands and face and brushes his teeth, then tucks him up and leaves a lamp on the floor by his head before rejoining the rest of us. 'He's only eight,' she explains for my benefit.

'How old are *you*?' It's out before I can stop it. The others're moving lamps onto two tables and setting up games of Ludo and Snakes and Ladders. Shrapnel throws me a glance that'd be a warning if it wasn't too late.

Ma arches her brow but answers. 'I'm fourteen, not that it's any of your business. Why?'

'I dunno: you seem so . . . grown up. When Bertie mentioned Ma, I expected someone old like my mum.'

'Yes, well, it's this war, Frecks. The bombing. People're getting killed or lost or wounded, and other people're having to take on responsibilities they didn't expect.' She smiles wryly. 'I was looking forward to being fourteen so I could get a job and go dancing at the Locarno. I never thought I'd be mother to seven kids: not yet anyway.'

I nod. 'I'm *really* grateful you let me stay, Ma. Victory Hall's so cool: like joining a family.'

'*Cool?* It's perishing *cold*, if you ask me.' She frowns. 'What're you, a flippin' Eskimo or something?'

Whoops. 'Er . . . cool's an expression me and my mates use, Ma: means good, nice – something that *feels* right.'

'I see. And where *are* your mates, Frecks?'

What do I say? They're in the year 2002? Yeah, right: how to get banished from Victory Hall in one easy lesson. I shrug. 'I dunno really: a long way from here.'

Her smile's wistful. 'The old, old story. Anyway, Frecks, *we're* your mates for the duration, as they say.'

'I know. Thanks.' I look at her. 'D'you *really* run this setup on fifteen bob a week, Ma, or do the kids . . . you know . . . nick stuff, like in *Oliver*?'

'Oliver?' Her face blanks, then grows indignant. 'Oliver *Twist*, you mean? No they do *not*, you cheeky young devil: or if they do they better not let *me* catch 'em at it. Listen.' She leans forward, stabs the air with a finger. 'I take a drop of Guinness and it makes me moody, but I'm *not* Mister Fagin. We get our grub by paying for it, same as everybody else. Anyone who nicks grub when there's a war on deserves to be shot.'

'I . . . I only meant . . .' *Why'd you ask that, you pathetic plonker?* My face feels like it's on fire. 'God, I'm *really* sorry . . . I don't know what made me *ask* that.' The games've stopped, everybody's staring at me. *You blew it: they're going to chuck you out.*

Ma makes light of it. 'It's all right, Frecks, no offence taken. We're none of us quite ourselves these days: it's the bombs. Why don't you go to bed, get a good night's sleep. You'll feel better in the morning.'

Her tone's gentle but I know I've hurt her. And the others, after all their kindness. It's a relief to step through the arch, away from their eyes. I stand at the foot of Spuggy's bed, undress by the meagre light from Mouse's lamp and skip the ablutions: don't have a toothbrush anyway. I spread the blanket and lie down. It feels funny without a pillow so I make a bundle of my clothes and lay my head on it. The blanket's thin and my feet're cold. What with that and the bombs and all the scary stuff that's using my brain for a race-track I don't expect to sleep, but in fact I go out like a light because the next thing I know I'm rubbing the grit out of my eyes and listening to the all-clear.

Twenty-Seven

I pretend to be asleep till everybody else is up. I dread facing them after what I said last night. I lie absolutely still as they splash about over the washbowls, dress and fold their blankets. As they move towards the arch a hand grabs my shoulder and Bertie growls, 'Shake a leg, Frecks: Ma's inspection in ten minutes.'

I've slept in my underpants like the other boys. I splash my face, dry it on a damp towel and get into my kit. Feels stupid, school uniform beside everybody else's tatty stuff. I look at the folded blankets and do mine the same. If I could think of something else to do I'd hang about in here a bit longer but there's nothing. I take a deep breath and walk through.

'Tea on the stove,' says Shrapnel. 'No milk, no sugar, help yourself.' They're sitting at the tables they played Ludo on last night, their hands curled round steaming mugs. A tin jug of tea simmers over a low flame. An empty mug stands next to the stove. I fill it and squeeze in between Shrapnel and Ma. Nobody gives me a funny look. Nobody mentions last night.

'No grub, I'm afraid,' says Ma.

I shrug. 'Tea's fine.'

'If we had some bacon,' says Wotsis gloomily, 'we could have bacon and eggs, if we had some eggs.' I laugh so suddenly tea comes down my nose. The others only smile, so I suppose they've heard it before. I wipe my dripping chin on my sleeve.

'That reminds me,' says Ma, ''berra find you a coat before you perish.' She drains her mug, gets up and goes through the arch.

'Did you fold your blanket, Frecks?' whispers Bertie.

'Yes.'

'Good job. Stickler for a folded blanket, is Ma.'

'What'd happen if . . .?'

'You'd find yourself washing the bedroom floor tonight on your hands and knees. She's a terror, 'specially when she's had a drink.'

'Does she *really* drink Guinness?'

'Not 'alf. Helps her cope, she reckons.'

'But she's only fourteen: how can she . . .?'

'No bovver. Old Rags brings it to her in the shop. When he can get it, that is.'

'Is that his name: Rags?'

Bertie shrugs. 'Who knows? It's what he calls hisself.'

Ma returns, nods. 'Good. Have you a comb, Frecks?'

'No, I never carry one.'

'There's one on the washstand. Use that till you get your own: you look like one of the Bisto Kids.'

'The *what*?'

She looks at me. 'Bisto Kids. You *know*, on the posters.'

'No.'

Everybody sniggers. Ma gives me a pitying look. 'Down to blast, I expect.'

'Pardon?'

She sighs. 'Never mind, I better be off.' She looks at Shrapnel. 'Look after 'em, all right?'

'Yes, Ma.'

Twenty-Eight

When Ma's gone, Shrapnel gives out jobs. Siren gets to wash the mugs, Mouse wipes. Nell and Bertie have to sweep both floors. Shrapnel pulls buckets from under the table, hands them to me and Wotsisname. 'Water,' he says. 'Show him where, Wotsis.'

We climb the steps. Wotsis sticks his head out, says 'All clear' and we emerge. 'Gorra watch out, see?' he explains. 'Grownups find out there's kids looking out for theirselves, have 'em in a home so fast their feet won't touch.'

I nod. 'And that's bad, is it?'

'Bad?' He looks at me. 'Ever *been* in a home, Frecks?'

'No.'

'They hits you for nuffink. Locks you up. Gives you porridge with black beetles in it. Mate of mine at school was in one; he told me.'

'What *about* school?'

'Shut 'cause of the bombing, fank God.'

It's a grey morning, dry with a sneaky wind. I button my blazer, hoping Ma'll remember about the coat. We cross the road, walk up a bit, turn left. A few of the houses here are flattened, some burned out; all are abandoned. Wotsis goes up to a green door that has a cardboard sign nailed to it. DANGER – UNEXPLODED BOMB. He opens the door and steps inside. I stop at the threshold, stuttering, pointing to the sign. He laughs, shakes his head. ''S not a *real* sign, Frecks: Shrapnel done it. Come on.' I follow him along a dim hallway into a kitchen that has a shallow stone sink and a brass tap. He clanks his bucket into the sink, turns on the tap. Water gushes. 'Mostly,' he explains, 'bombing breaks the pipes, and if it don't they comes from the corporation and turns the water off.' He grins. 'Forgot this one though, and that's good for us. Sign'll keep 'em off, bit of luck.'

When both buckets are full we carry them back along the hallway. Wotsis inches the door open and peers out. 'All clear.' We leave.

Water's unbelievably heavy. We stagger along, leaving a trail of splashes. By the time we've manoeuvred the buckets into the hole and down the steps they're about a quarter empty. We teem the precious stuff into the zinc tank, and Shrapnel says we'll have to go again. This time he comes with us, bringing a third bucket. Limping back that second time, I remember a TV programme we watched at school about how people in the Third World have to spend most of each day carrying water. I'd been like, *So flipping what?* but these two journeys make me realise how important piped water is. I think maybe we could try carrying the buckets on our heads like they do in Africa, but then I realise a line of kids walking down the street with buckets on their heads might attract the sort of attention we want to avoid, so I kick it into touch.

Twenty-Nine

Chamber-pots is easily the worst chore. Well, think about it: eight people stuck in a cellar twelve hours at a stretch. I won't go on but the thing is, Shrapnel always sees to it himself. Ma leaves him in charge, he could give anybody else the job but he never does. 'That's why we foller's 'im,' says Wotsis. 'Respec'.' He doesn't tell me where Shrapnel empties the pots and I don't ask.

Once Victory Hall's spick and span, we go outside. The sky to the north is hazy with smoke from last night's fires. The docks're that way, they've had the worst of the bombing. Shrapnel gazes north. 'Take 'em to the park, Nell,' he says. 'I'm off up the docks.'

Nell's oldest after Shrapnel. We follow her while he goes off by himself. Mouse is trotting beside me.

'Why's Shrapnel going to the docks?' I ask.

'He's after stuff for his c'llection.'

'What sort of stuff?'

'Shrapnel, of course. Bomb tails. Don't you know *any*fing?'

I shrug. 'Not a lot, Mouse.'

''S why he's *called* Shrapnel, you donkey.'

'Right.' *Cheeky little brat.*

In the park Nell and Bertie pick sides. There's only two each so it doesn't take long. I end up with Mouse and Bertie and we're the Germans. Nell's got Siren and Wotsisname and they're the English. We play at Invasion. The bandstand's England. We have to try to capture the bandstand while Nell's gang defends it. It's all a bit tame, not a patch on creeping, but these kids're the only mates I've got here in 1940 so I get into it, shooting from behind benches, making dashes when nobody's looking. I'm starving, but the game takes my mind off my stomach for a while.

Everything goes smoothly till me and Mouse and Bertie take the bandstand. It's dead easy, because Wotsis gets a splinter in his palm and Nell and Siren rush to see what he's yelling about. While they're busy I shout, 'Go!' We charge up the steps, grab the two girls from behind and wrestle them to the floor where Mouse and Bertie sit on them while I caper about, doing Hitler salutes.

Nell goes ape-shape. 'The Germans don't *win*!' she screeches, bucking and writhing till Bertie's dislodged and she scrambles to her feet. Teeth bared, she thrusts her scarlet features in my face. 'It's *your* fault,' she shrieks. 'You don't know how to *play* properly.'

It's amazing, I can't believe it: talk about *overreact*. I back up, hands raised. 'OK, OK, don't get your knickers in a twist, it's only a *game*.' I'm laughing – can't help it. It's her face, you should've *seen* it; like I've murdered her flipping *mother* or something. And my laughing makes her even madder.

'Don't say "knickers", you rude beggar,' she cries. 'And it *isn't* just a game: there's a *war* on. You're a . . . a *squanderbug*!'

That does it: squanderbug. I'm laughing so hard my knees won't hold me up. I drop to the boards and kneel, clutching myself, fighting to breathe as tears roll down my cheeks. She's prancing round me, kicking me in the back and sides, yelling and screeching. I'd stop if I could but I can't. *Squanderbug.*

Then something awful happens. Really, really awful. One minute I'm laughing so hard I damn near christen my shorts, and the next I'm crying. And I don't mean just sobbing either. I mean suddenly I'm *roaring*: rocking with my face in my hands while these harsh, animal noises I can't believe I'm making come blaring out of my mouth. I've no control: I can feel the others in a ring round me, staring, and Nell's gone quiet but I can't close my mouth or stop the noise coming out. A soupy jumble of images bubbles inside my skull: Pete and Danny, Eden Camp, old Coverley. A pale small hand in a heap of rubble. Mum. I kneel and roar, on and on and on.

Thirty

'What's going on here?' Gruff voice, tall dark figure warped through tears.

One of the kids, Mouse, I think, grabs my shoulder and shakes it, going, 'It's all right, Frecks, we're not mad wiv you, *honest*.'

Somebody else says, 'It's nuffink, mister, we was just playing and he got upset.'

'Hmm.' The figure bends over me. 'All right, are you, lad?'

Oh yeah, I'm all right. Never been better. I'm only sixty-two years away from home, aching for a mother who hasn't been born yet, in a place where you need papers to stay alive and I haven't got any, where everybody's got a gas mask except me. Apart from that, and the fact that I'm cold and hungry and you're a policeman, I'm fine, absolutely fine.

A policeman. I grit my teeth, clench my fists. *Stop crying, you wuss, get a grip.* I can't afford to be questioned, taken to a police station. I make a stupendous effort, bring myself under control. 'Y-yes, officer, I'm all right. I got upset, that's all.'

I'm wiping my eyes with the sleeve of my blazer when he goes, 'Hello: what's *this*?' He takes hold of my wrist, turns it, peers at my watch. *Digital* watch. I better think fast.

'It's a watch,' I croak. My throat's clogged. 'Special one. My uncle got it in America.'

'America. How's it work, then?'

I show him, trying to keep my hands from shaking. The kids're interested too. I haven't deliberately hidden my watch from them until now: it just never occurred to me, though I realise it *should* have. Nobody's noticed it before, that's all.

'Hmmm.' The constable looks impressed. 'Queer notions them Yanks come out with: Spam, powdered eggs and now a watch with no hands.' He chuckles. 'It'll be aeroplanes without propellers next, I shouldn't wonder.'

I shake my head. '*We* get them before the Yanks.' What an incredibly silly thing to say, but it just slips out: it's impossible to watch every word.

Luckily he takes it as a joke. 'You're probably right, lad: a country that'll paint the tops of its pillar-boxes yellow as a way of detecting poison gas might do *anything*. Anyway,' he peers at me, 'you seem to be over your little upset, so I'll be on my way.' He treats us all to a stern look. 'Mind how you go, now.'

I nearly burst out laughing as he goes down the steps. I didn't realise policemen actually used to *say* that.

It's nearly as funny as squanderbug.

Thirty-One

We stand watching the policeman walk away. I'm feeling dead embarrassed about breaking down like that: they'll think Nell's screeching got to me. I have to patch up my cred. 'Uh . . . sorry about that, guys. Stuff's happened to me, y'know? Bad stuff. Sneaks up on me now and then.'

Nell nods without looking at me. 'Know wotcha mean, Frecks. I cries for hours sometimes, in bed. We *all* do, even Ma. It's this rotten war.'

'Yeah,' agrees Bertie, 'so don't fret, Frecks.' He grins. 'But remember, when we play Invasion us Germans don't win.'

I nod. '*Verstehen.*'

'You what?'

'I understand.'

'Ah.'

'I'm *flipping* hungry,' goes Mouse. 'My stomach finks my froat's cut.' The others groan their sympathy.

Seeing a chance to repair my image, I'm like, 'I know a bunch of guys might feed us.' I nod towards the path I took the day before yesterday, which feels like a hundred years ago.

'Guys?' Nell frowns. 'What *sort* of guys?'

'We can't beg,' puts in Bertie. 'Ma says we're not to beg.'

I shake my head. 'We won't *beg*, we'll ask.'

'That's different, is it?' says Wotsis.

'*Course* it's different,' insists Mouse. 'Begging's begging, asking's just asking. *Everybody* knows that.'

I lead the way. When we come in sight of the emplacement Nell stops dead. 'Soldiers? We can't go near soldiers, Frecks.'

'Why not?'

''Cause they're part of . . . you know: *them*.'

'I don't know what you mean, Nell.'

'You *do*: them that wants to shove us all in homes. They'll snitch on us.'

I shake my head. 'No they won't, they're mates of mine. I'll go first, you wait here.'

She sighs. 'There's *six* of us, Frecks. They can't feed six of us out of their bleat'n rations, they'll tell you to buzz off.'

Too ravenous to stand arguing, I leave the cover of the trees and set off across the grass. Five pairs of hungry eyes watch from the shadows.

Thirty-Two

''S not *today*, is it?' The one I call Cheese Roll grins as I approach. The guy's polishing the mechanism, tidying the emplacement.

'Sorry?'

'The film. They're not shooting today, I hope – we've an inspection in an hour: top brass.'

'Oh.' I smile. 'No, it's after the war.'

'Hear that, lads?' The other four turn. 'We're not to be famous till after the war.'

'Drat!' growls Redhead. 'And here I was thinking I'd be taking tea with Vera Lynn any day now.' He looks at me. 'Can't you have a word, son, gee 'em up a bit?'

I smile again, shake my head. I don't blame them for taking the mickey, but I doubt if I've ever felt less like joshing. I don't feel like asking for grub either, but I opened my big mouth in front of the kids and I'm stuck with it. 'I . . . was wondering if there's any chance of some grub.'

Cheese Roll shakes his head. 'Sorry, son, it's like I said: we've a big inspection this morning, the ladies don't come round.'

'Oh.'

My face must've dropped 'cause Redhead says, 'I think there's a square or two of chocolate in my side-pack if it'll help.'

I smile at him. 'Thanks, that's great, but it isn't just me.' I look towards the path. The kids have crept forward a bit.

Redhead looks. '*Six* of you? He looks at me sharply. 'Are you a *family* or what? You can't just . . .'

'Yes, I suppose we *are* a sort of family. We look after one another. We're all right, it's just . . . grub's hard to get sometimes, y'know?'

'Have you got ration books? Money? How d'you *live*, son?'

'We manage.' Nell's stopped the kids coming closer. 'Look, I'm sorry: I shouldn't have come here. We'll go. Thanks for . . .'

'Hey, hey, not so fast.' Cheese Roll lays a hand on my shoulder, not to stop me, more to slow me down. 'I reckon between us we might rustle up a bit of something just this once, but you know, you're kids, and if there's nobody to look after you you'd be better going to one of the rest centres, let 'em find you somewhere to live. Winter's coming: try sleeping rough then and you'll perish.' He removes his hand, looks at his mates. 'How about it, lads: tin of bully, a biscuit or two? We must have *something* salted away.'

I get the feeling one or two of the men would like to chase us off: grub's in short supply for them too, but Cheese Roll's the one with the stripe on his arm and they move towards the tent they're living in to see what they can find. I beckon the kids and they waste no time.

There's a tin of Spam and another of evaporated milk, some biscuits in a paper bag and two bars of chocolate, one partly eaten. There's ten smokes too, but Cheese Roll grabs them back, shaking his head and tutting at the guy who offers them. 'You can't eat here,' he growls, puncturing the tins for us with his jack knife, 'we've bulled up.'

We grab the stuff, thank him and the others and turn to go. Cheese Roll catches my arm. 'Now don't forget what I told you, son: get these kids to a rest centre, sooner the better.'

I nod without promising. When I look back he's watching. I wave and hurry into the trees.

Thirty-Three

We sit on a bench by the bandstand and share out the loot. It isn't a pig-out. Nell uses the sharp lid of the spam tin to cut the meat into six slices so we've got one each. There are twelve squares of chocolate, which comes to two apiece. The paper bag holds nine biscuits: one and a half each. We've no cups, so the milk tin goes along the row and everybody has a suck, and another when it comes back. I suppose some people have a harder suck than others, but everybody watches everybody else and I don't think there's any cheating. We even take turns dabbing crumbs out of the corners of the biscuit bag with a wet finger. I could murder a hot'n'spicy pizza with extra pepperoni and an order of garlic bread, but I daren't let my mind go too far down that particular road: I've cried enough for one day.

Like I said, it's not a pig-out, but we feel better for it and keep ourselves amused in various ways for the rest of the day. At one point we form a line and we're marching along a footpath belting out a song I've never heard of about something called the Siegfried Line when we meet two women coming the other way. One of them glares at us and goes, 'Ssssh! It's *Sunday*.'

The song tails off and we march in silence till we're well past them. A thought occurs to me. 'Hey, Nell: how come Ma's working on a Sunday?'

She snorts. 'Sunday's just another day to old Rags, Frecks: he's not a Christian.'

'What *is* he, then?'

'Jew.'

'Ah, so he has *Fridays* off, or is it Saturdays?'

'He has *no* day off, the money-grubbing blighter: seven days a week, that's Rags. Only fing he does is jack in work early on Fridays. Oh, and he once bit Ma's head off 'cause she asked him if he'd fetch her a pie to go wiv her stout. Apart from that and sounding foreign he's just like any ovver geezer, except he's stingy o' course. Hey, listen: d'you know why a fruppenny bit's got twelve sides?'

'No.' I've actually been wondering ever since I first saw this odd-looking coin.

Nell grins. 'So you can get it out of a Jew's fist wiv a spanner.'

Everybody laughs. I don't think they've heard of racism in 1940, but surely they've heard of concentration camps and you'd think *that'd* make a difference. Anyway I'm in no position to protest so I laugh along with 'em, uneasily.

'He's out all day,' continues Nell, 'leaves Ma to run the shop. I'd tell him what he could do wiv his old job if it was me.'

'Good job it *isn't* you then, Nell,' puts in Wotsis, 'or what would happen to us? No grub, nowhere to kip. We'd all be in flipping *homes*, that's what.'

'Yes, all *right*, Wots. I didn't mean . . . we'd be done for without Ma's fifteen bob, I know that: I only meant he *uses* her, takes advantage. Didn't ought to take advantage when there's a war on: it's unwhatsit – patriotic.'

She avoids anyone coming back at her by starting up another song. 'Quartermaster's Store', this one's called. I know the tune but not the words. There are loads of verses. We're still singing it, marching in line, when we cross Southwark Park Road. There aren't many people about, but the few we pass probably think we're barmy.

Thirty-Four

We're back before the sirens but Ma's there already, so's Shrapnel. He's peeling spuds, she's yelling at him for leaving eyes in. We're supposed to avoid attracting attention, but we can hear Ma from across the road. I start to mention it on the steps but Nell kicks my leg and hisses, 'Leave it: she's had a drink.'

The sirens go. We set the tables, quietly so we won't upset Ma, who's gone through to her bedroom. When everything's ready we sit, listening for planes and waiting for the pan of spuds to boil. I'm on edge in case somebody tells Ma I asked the searchlight crew for grub: I don't want to add begging to last night's crack about Oliver.

She appears after a while, and I think she's had a lie down because she's looking a bit more cheerful. Better still from my point of view, she's carrying a heavy coat over her arm. She throws it at me. 'Here y'are, Frecks: try this for size.'

I catch it, put it on. It's a typical Thirties item: big shoulders, wide lapels, long skirt, flipping *belt*. I can't see myself but I must look like something out of one of those black–and–white gangster movies. George Raft, maybe. All that's missing is the fedora, gun in the pocket, but hey: it's thick, it's warm, it reaches down to my ankles and it comes with a gas mask. I plunge my arms in the pockets and grin at Ma. 'Thanks, Ma, it's absolutely *wizard*.' I actually remember to say 'wizard' and not 'ace' or 'wicked'.

She smiles. 'You look even more like a Bisto Kid now but looks don't matter: it's warmth that counts.'

I keep it on, eat dinner in it. If you can call two watery spuds dinner. I don't want to sound ungrateful: without Ma there'd be no dinner at all, and even she can't get us meat without a ration book. I know all this. It's just that potatoes by themselves don't exactly excite the palate, especially if there isn't any salt, which there isn't. I look at these two bluish-whitish lumps steaming on my plate and imagine them swimming in a sea of my mum's gravy, alongside a generous wedge of steak and kidney pie and a double scoop of baby garden peas, and my stomach yearns.

I sit there in my gangster coat, chewing mush and looking forward to a long evening of Snakes and Ladders, and an all-too-familiar feeling creeps over me. I know it's a funny thing to say with enemy aircraft overhead and bombs falling and buildings blazing less than half a mile away but there's no getting away from it.

I'm *bored*.

Thirty-Five

'Ma?' It's ten o'clock. The others are getting ready for bed except Mouse, who's been asleep hours.

Ma's got a comb and toothbrush for me somewhere. She looks up from rummaging in her bag. 'What?'

'D'you think I could start helping you at Mr Rags's?'

'Ha!' She snorts. 'Breaks his heart to pay *me*, Frecks: he'd never take on a second assistant as long as I'm coping.'

I shake my head. 'I wouldn't want paying, Ma. It'd be something to do, that's all. And company for you.'

She looks at me. 'What's up? Aren't you getting on with the others?'

'Oh yeah, we get on fine, only I've not been used to playing. My folks had a shop, see. I helped when I wasn't at school.' *What a liar.*

'Ah. And you're missing it, I expect.'

'Well yeah: missing *everything*. So I just thought . . .'

'I know. Trouble is, I can't see old Rags agreeing, Frecks. He'd imagine us gossiping instead of getting on with our work. Tell you what, though.'

'What?'

'If you could find your way by yourself, you could come after he's gone out. He's hardly ever in after ten o'clock, and as long as you left by about three he'd be none the wiser.'

'Could you draw me a rough map, Ma, here to Tower Bridge?'

''Spect so. D'you want to try tomorrow?'

'Great, if that's all right.'

She frowns. 'Y'know, Frecks, I can't help thinking there's something funny about you. The way you talk, like somebody on the pictures. "Yeah", you say, and "Great". Not to mention "cool". Are you mad on American pictures, is that it?'

I nod and grin. 'Yeah, Ma, that's it. You've sussed my little secret.' I'm not surprised she thinks I talk funny: I've noticed the difference myself, the way our speech has become Americanised over the years. I'd modify it if I could: talk like the others, but it's impossible. I'd have to analyse every sentence before I said it.

She smiles. 'We'll have to go to the Trocette sometime, Frecks, or the Rialto: when they're showing something good.'

I nod. 'That'd be great, Ma. Look forward to it.' *See George Raft in this coat, probably*.

'Here.' She's found the comb and toothbrush.

I take them, tell her she shouldn't, not on fifteen bob a week.

She scoffs. 'I'd sooner spend the money than have you running round looking like an urchin, showing me up.'

She's fourteen, talks forty, but I aren't half glad I found her. I treat my teeth to a really good scrub before getting into bed. Comb my hair, too, which probably proves I'm three parts daft.

Should be good tomorrow.

Thirty-Six

One good thing about waiting till after ten is that I can help with the chores. Me and Wotsis get the water job again. We spill some, same as yesterday, and this time Shrapnel doesn't volunteer to help so we end up going three times. A cold wind italicises the smoke from last night's fires and scrapes dead leaves along the gutter. I'm glad of my coat.

Everybody thinks I'm potty wanting to work in Rags's shop. 'Don't you see how *dreary* it'll be?' goes Siren, wrinkling up her nose. 'Smelly old geezers pawing through smelly old clothes?'

'It's inside though,' I counter. 'At least I'll be warm.'

'Aw, you *will*, Frecks,' chuckles Bertie. 'There's none so warm as the lousy, my grandad says. *Said*,' he amends, smile fading.

'Each to his own, *my* grandad says,' growls Nell, 'so we'll leave you to it, Frecks. Give Ma our love, won'tcha?'

Tooley Street, the shop's in. I set off northwards, stopping every few minutes to consult Ma's sketch map. Once, I catch sight of myself in a shop window and think, *If I walked through Witchfield looking like this people'd bump into lamp-posts, staring.* As it is nobody spares me a glance. One big store I pass *has* no windows: bomb-blast blown them all in. Girls with brooms are sweeping shards into glittering piles. Somebody has pinned this notice to the door: MORE OPEN THAN USUAL. I have to laugh.

Soon I spot the towers and know I'm close. I look at my watch. Three minutes to. Ma's told me she'll stand in the doorway dead on ten. If she shakes her head it'll mean Rags is in and I must walk by, try again in half an hour. If she doesn't, the coast is clear.

I turn into Tooley Street and spot the shop straight away. It's on the other side. There's a wire rack outside with beat-up shoes and boots, and a small grimy window criss-crossed with the usual sticky tape. As I dawdle towards it, a clock starts striking. The shop door opens and there's Ma. She spots me and doesn't shake her head so I cross. She smiles, steps to one side and says, 'Come into my parlour.'

And that's how the real fun begins.

Thirty-Seven

Jeez, what a dump! I don't know how anybody can bear to *live* like that. The second I cross the threshold the pong hits me. Mildewed kit, of course: I expected *that*. But there are other smells: old fat, bad drains, the fungal reek of rotting wood. I pull a face. 'Stinks in here, Ma: how d'you *stand* it?'

Ma shrugs, closing the door. 'No choice, have I, Frecks? Need the wage, got no address, no papers, no nothing. His nibs pays me, asks no questions. Besides, I've got used to it: don't even notice it now.'

She shows me round. Hardly any light makes it through the mucky window: it's like being underwater. The shop itself has a battered counter with drawers in it and shelves behind going right to the ceiling with stuff folded on them: socks, mufflers, underwear that might have been stripped off dead tramps, shirts, collars – tat like that. There's a step-ladder for reaching the high shelves. The rest of the floorspace is taken up with tubular racks on wheels, their rails crammed with hangers. From these hangers, like the victims of mass execution, hang suits, trousers, coats, jackets, skirts, dresses and weird bits I can't even identify. If they were mine I'd cart the whole lot off to the dump and bribe the guy in charge to please let me put them in his nice clean skip. As it is, I can't imagine what'd drive anybody to *touch* the stuff without rubber gloves and a gas mask, let alone buy it.

Through a sticky bead curtain lies the other downstairs room. *Room*'s the wrong word because there isn't any room. Apart from the corner with a sink and a gas ring and the narrow gangway that leads to it, the place is crammed with tea-chests and packing-cases, all brimming with stuff you can't believe people once admired themselves in mirrors wearing. To drink a cup of tea you either stand in the gangway or, if you don't care what the seat of your pants touches, sit on one of the chests.

Upstairs is just one big room, full of kit I wouldn't bury a dog in. The stairs themselves creak and sag underfoot so that although a second, narrower flight leads to the attic where Mr Rags lives, Ma has never risked it and I don't fancy it either.

Outside over the shop a faded sign reads: GOOD-AS-NEW APPAREL FOR THE DISCERNING. It's a lie Herr Doktor Goebbels would be proud of.

Thirty-Eight

'Now,' goes Ma, rubbing her hands together, 'prices.'

'You mean we *charge* for this stuff?' I'm joking, but I mean . . .

''*Course*, mutton-head: Rags got to live, ain't he?'

'I suppose.'

'Righto. Well, there's two sorts of customers: them that wants to buy, and them that wants to swop.'

'*Swop?*'

'Oh yeah: lots of people bring something to swop – something they've worn till they're sick of it. Don't have the coupons for *new*, see, so they settle for the next best thing, which is something *different*.'

'Right.' I'd go nude first, but I don't say it.

'If there's no swop it goes like this: everything on these racks here,' she points to the first row, 'is a shilling. Don't matter what it is, it's a shilling. Row behind, a tanner. Back row, thruppence.'

'OK.' I know old money now, so this is no prob. 'What about swops, Ma?'

'Ah.' She thinks for a moment. 'If you get a swop, Frecks, better show me: just till you learn what to allow.' She smiles. 'Geezers'll try it on, see: bring some old rag and want a bob off a fur coat.'

'Fur coat?' Only fur coats around here are on the rats.

She grins. 'Joking. We have *some* good stuff though: look at your coat.'

I'm trying *not* to look at it: don't want to think of it hanging here.

We're not overrun with the discerning and, anyway, Ma doesn't let me loose on the customers, first day. I just watch what goes off the racks and replace it with stuff from the back room when the customer's gone. Half the time she makes me take it away and fetch something else, but I reckon I'll get the hang of it eventually and it beats playing in the park, even *with* the stink. Fact is, by the time she makes me leave at three I've stopped noticing the smell. I disappear into my shilling coat and dawdle back the way I came, past pasty-faced mothers and knots of foreign soldiers. It's chilly, the trees are almost bare. Ma says if the bombers come tonight it'll be the twentieth night in a row. I can't see anyone throwing a party to mark the occasion.

Thirty-Nine

'Where's Shrapnel?' Eyes everywhere, Ma. Spots he's missing when she's still on the stairs, tired though she is.

'He went down the biscuits,' says Nell.

'Peek Freans?'

'Yeah.'

'How long ago?'

Nell shrugs. 'Dunno. Half-hour, mebbe.' She looks round. 'Anyone notice what time Shrapnel went out? What about you, Frecks, fancy American watch?'

I shake my head. 'Sorry, I was busy with Aladdin here.' Aladdin's what they call the stove: it's an Aladdin stove.

Nobody's sure how long Shrapnel's been gone. Ma plonks a loaf of bread on the table. She's worried because it's coming up to six, time for the sirens. 'I hope he won't be daft enough to try to get back through the bombing,' she growls. I smell stout on her breath.

'He won't, Ma,' soothes Siren, 'he's got more sense. He'll go to the nearest shelter, wait till morning.'

'Scoff all the bleat'n biscuits hisself,' grumbles Bertie.

Ma flares up. 'Wouldn't *be* no bleat'n biscuits without Shrapnel, Bertie, so you can shut your trap, fetch the bread-knife and slice this loaf. And let's have the slices *straight* for once.'

We hear the first planes at ten to seven. Shrapnel hasn't returned. 'That's it, then,' sighs Ma, 'something *else* for me to worry about.' There are black circles under her eyes, she looks wrecked. I don't understand why she bothers with us lot, I'm just glad she does.

'Don't worry, Ma,' murmurs Nell. 'He's in a shelter somewhere, nibbling Teddy Bear biscuits, having a good old sing-song. He'll turn up for breakfast, you'll see.'

He doesn't though. When the all-clear wakes us at six and we roll out of our beds, his hasn't been slept in. When I've got the stove lit and put water on for tea, he's still missing. And when we sit in the clammy half-light, warming our hands on our mugs, Shrapnel isn't among us. We don't know it yet but he'll never be here again. I'll tell you why, but I warn you, it's a *real* war story, the sort they never show on telly. Skip the next bit if you like: I won't blame you.

Forty

Ma sets off for work at half seven, dead worried. Ten minutes later, when Nell's dishing out jobs, she's back, standing on the steps with clenched fists and a chalk-white face. We all know something's wrong and we go quiet, watching her.

'He's not back then?' Her voice scrapes like dead leaves blowing.

Nell shakes her head, murmurs, 'What's up, Ma?'

'People're saying Stainer Street arch got a direct hit. *Hundreds* dead. I bet Shrapnel . . .' She can't go on. Her face twists up, she starts to cry.

Nell puts an arm round her, guides her to a chair, looks at me. 'Light the stove, Frecks, warm up that char.' She's kneeling, holding both Ma's hands between her own, rubbing them. Ma's shaking, making mewing noises. I hurry to do as Nell says. The others move about quietly, starting their jobs.

It must be rotten tea warmed up like that, but Ma takes the mug I offer, cries into it, takes the occasional sip. It's got all the sugar we had, about three spoonfuls, stirred into it. For the shock, Nell explains.

It works, because after a bit Ma starts fretting about her job. 'Rags'll think I'm a shirker,' she sniffles. 'He'll sack me, *then* what will we do?'

I see a chance to be useful for once. 'What if I go and see him, Ma? Explain. I could even offer to stand in for you.'

'No.' She shakes her head. 'He mustn't know I've had you in the shop, Frecks. Go see him though, tell him about . . . Stainer

89

Street. Say . . . oh, I don't know: say my *brother* was under the arch. He doesn't know anything about me: doesn't know I haven't *got* a brother. Tell him I'll be in tomorrow.'

I get my coat, leave with Wotsis, who's off by himself for water. Outside I catch his sleeve. 'What's Stainer Street arch, Wotsis?'

'Railway arch.' He nods westward. 'That way. They use it for a shelter.' He looks at me. 'Shrapnel's not *bound* to've been there though, is he, Frecks?'

I shake my head. ''Course not, could be anywhere. I'll go that way round and have a look, but don't tell Ma.'

I walk west till I come to the railway, then follow it north towards the worst sight I'll ever see in my life.

Forty-One

I won't go into details: I don't think I could. I'll just say what happened and you'll probably be able to imagine the rest.

A high embankment carries the railway across the bit of London we're living in. It's a wide embankment because there are a lot of lines, and in some places viaducts carry the lines over roads, streams and so on. The width of the tracks makes the viaduct arches wide too, and people have taken to using some of them as bomb shelters. It's not a bad idea: brick walls on two sides, six feet of ballast, clay and earth overhead. Being open at both ends they tend to be a bit draughty but they're better than nothing, and not everybody can find a place in a street shelter or Underground station.

Last night, the night of Monday 7 October 1940, every square inch of ground under the Stainer Street arch was occupied. Some people had brought mattresses and bedding, some had chairs or boxes, others just sat or lay on the ground wrapped in blankets, coats or whatever they had. Sacks, some had round them. There were hundreds sheltering there. I didn't know any of this at the time, of course: I'd never even heard of Stainer Street. I read about it in Tuesday night's paper, where it appeared under a big black headline. By then I'd been to Stainer Street and was wishing I hadn't.

What happened was, a bomb landed on the railway track on top of the viaduct, and it must have been a special sort of bomb, because instead of detonating when it hit the track it came straight through and exploded inside the arch. It was a terrific explosion, and the blast was directed inwards and down by the roof and walls, so that the people got the full force of it and were blown to pieces. This was in the early hours, and when I got there around eight, teams of rescuers were still bringing out stretcherfuls of mangled remains. The police had thrown a cordon round the scene to keep gawpers away, but I was close enough to see rows of shapeless humps under bloody sheets and a rescue worker throwing up beside an ambulance. And yes, one of those humps was Shrapnel. At least one.

How did I find out? By a miracle of sorts. I mean, it was to be a week before the authorities were able to say how many had been under that arch, and to identify most of them. Some were never identified, because thieves had got there before the police and stripped them of their papers and ration books. Hard to believe, but it happened a lot in the Blitz.

Anyway I'm standing at a barrier, gazing at the scene and thinking about Shrapnel when a voice I recognise says, 'Bet they never make a film about *this*.' It's Cheese Roll, with brick-dust all over his uniform and cuts on his hands. He's obviously been helping.

I shake my head. 'Don't think so.'

He looks at me. 'This is no place for a kid, and I thought I told you to go to a rest centre.'

'I know, but I'm looking for somebody.'

'Who?'

'Mate of mine. We think he might have sheltered here last night.'

'I hope not, son. What's he look like, your mate?'

I shrug. 'He's twelve, a bit taller than me, black hair. Calls himself Shrapnel.'

'Hmm. Why d'you think he might have sheltered here?'

'He went out around five yesterday to see someone at Peek Freans. That's near here, isn't it?'

Cheese Roll nods. 'Down the road.' His voice sounds funny. I look at him and he says, 'Why Peek Freans, son, do'you know?'

I nod. 'Yes, he knows a man there, gets biscuits. Broken ones.'

'Ah.'

'What?'

'Look.' He lays an arm across my shoulders, steers me away from the onlookers. 'I can't be sure, and I hope I'm wrong, but I think your mate Shrapnel *might* have been under that arch.'

'H-how d'you know?'

'Well, me and my crew were brought in at six this morning to help look for survivors. We didn't find anybody alive, worse luck, but we found . . . something funny. I don't *mean* funny, I mean strange. There was a lad, trousers half-down: blast plays tricks like that, y'know. And inside his trousers, tied to a bit of string round his waist, were two flour-bags full of broken biscuits.'

'Oh.' I clutch Cheese Roll's hand, can't help it. I feel like I felt in the bandstand: bursting with something inside that'll come out roaring.

He squeezes my shoulder. 'Steady, old chap.' I bite my lip, swallow the lump in my throat. 'Good man.' He leads me to a low wall, sits me down, hands me a big khaki handkerchief. I dab my eyes, wipe my nose. 'Better?' I nod. He gives me a minute, then says, 'Sounds like your mate, doesn't it? I'm sorry.'

I shake my head. 'Not bound to be. Plenty of guys could have biscuits. It might be the Peek Freans man: you know – the one Shrapnel was meeting?'

'Ah, there's another thing.' Cheese Roll's tone is soft, but I know he doesn't want to leave me clutching at straws. 'Shrapnel: how did the lad come by a name like that, eh?'

'He collects it. Collects shrapnel.'

'I guessed that was it.' He sits down beside me. 'The lad we found: his pockets were bulging with shrapnel.' He shakes his

head. 'I'm afraid you're going to have to let your mate go, son.'
He stands, looks down at me. 'If it's any consolation, he never
knew what hit him. None of them did.'

And that's how I found out. It wasn't the only thing I found
out that morning, but it was the most important thing at the
time. I gave Cheese Roll his hankie back and set off to confront
Mr Rags. I didn't feel like it, but there must have been thousands
of people in London that morning dragging themselves off to do
things they didn't feel like doing.

C'est la guerre, as the French say.

Forty-Two

It's a quarter to nine when I turn into Tooley Street. As soon as I see the shop I spot its owner. He's on the step, fidgeting, peering up and down the street. He's a little guy, nearly bald, with wire-rimmed glasses and a straggly ginger moustache that looks like a caterpillar crawled out of his nose and died. He's wearing a shiny three-piece suit off the sixpenny rack. As I cross over he looks at his watch.

'Mr Rags?'

'Yes, what is it?' Pale eyes behind blue-tinted lenses.

'My name's Frecks. I've come with a message from . . . your assistant.' It's only when I start speaking that I realise I don't know Ma's name. She'd hardly be Ma to her boss.

'From Sandra? How do you know her?'

'We're cousins. She can't come today: her brother's been killed.' I feel uncomfortable, like I'm using Shrapnel's death in some shameful way.

Rags frowns. 'Killed: where? How old was he? I didn't know she had a brother.'

'She had one. Lewis, twelve. He was under the Stainer Street arch. It was bombed. Everybody was killed.'

He nods. 'Yes, I have heard. Stainer Street. How sad for Sandra. Well.' He sounds more irritated than sorry. 'It can't be helped, I will have to manage alone. Tell your cousin I'm sorry, and I will expect her tomorrow.'

Not, *Tell her to take as long as she needs*, then? Anger surges in me: I want to shout at this shabby little man that she'll be back when she feels like it, but I control myself. I'm already going to have to tell Ma about Shrapnel: I don't want to have to say I lost her her job as well. I repeat the word *tomorrow* as contemptuously as I dare and turn my back on him.

Forty-Three

It's rotten, making my way back to Victory Hall, thinking what to say. How to break the bad news, wondering how Ma'll take it. I even think of not going back. London's a big place – I could find another district: cross the river so they'd never find me.

I don't, though, and the shameful thing is this: it isn't a sense that I owe it to Ma and the others not to chicken out that draws me back; it's my bed, my grub. It's having a sort of home, a sort of family.

Ma's on the sofa, and I can tell when I'm halfway down the steps she knows I've been to Stainer Street. Wotsis must've told her. She stands up, peering into my face. 'He's gone, hasn't he?' I nod. I can't speak round the lump in my throat. I'm not a hugger but a nod's not enough. I wrap my arms round her and bury my face in her hair. We're both crying. The others stand silent, watching us. Ma gets a grip before I do, gently pushes me away, blows into a hanky, says in a husky voice, 'This won't get the baby bathed.' I've never heard this expression before but I know what it means: it means crying won't bring Shrapnel back, and it'll stop us doing what has to be done. I haven't got a hanky so I use the sleeve of my beautiful coat.

Everybody's sniffling a bit. Ma fills the jug with water from the tank, lights Aladdin, sets the jug on top. 'What *we* need,' she husks, 'is a nice mug of char.' We need a lot of other things as well: money, ration books, proper homes – we need our *mums*, but we can actually *give* ourselves a nice mug of char and we do. It makes us feel less helpless.

As we sit and sip, Ma asks how I know about Shrapnel. I tell her about Cheese Roll. When I get to the bit about the flour-bags she makes a small sound in her throat and nods, staring at the floor. 'That settles it then,' she murmurs. 'That's how he carried them.'

Nobody talks for a bit, then Ma remembers the reason I went out in the first place. 'See old Rags, did you, Frecks?'

'Yes, Ma, and he wants strangling if you ask me. He's sorry, and he'll expect you tomorrow. How sorry's *that*?'

Ma shrugs. 'He's all right, Frecks. Bit tight but he took me on, no papers, no questions asked. It isn't everybody'd do that, especially with a war on.'

'Well, I think you're entitled to a week off at least, brother killed like that.'

'Shrapnel wasn't my *brother*, Frecks.'

'No, but Rags doesn't know that: it'd be all the same if you *had* lost your brother.'

Ma looks at me, nods. 'Yes, it *would* be the same, Frecks: there'd be things to do, money to earn, same as usual. A war to win. People everywhere are losing people, and if they all took a week off the Thames'd be full of U-boats in a jiffy. So I'll be there tomorrow, bright and early, doing my little bit. Of course,' she adds, '*you* needn't come if you don't want to: there'll be plenty to do here now we're seven instead of eight.'

I'll be there too, but not for Rags *or* to do my little bit. I'll be there for Ma, because she's there for me.

Forty-Four

Nell's stepped into Shrapnel's shoes so you'd hardly see the join. Gives out the jobs, does the chamber-pots herself. Fetching water in the rain I ask Wotsis. 'What happened to Spuggy?'

He looks at me sharply. 'How d'you know about Spuggy?'

'Mouse told me I got his bed.'

'Yeah, you did. Strange kid, Spuggy.'

'How d'you mean?'

'Had a fing about being shut in: couldn't stand it. Ma had endless bovver wiv him: keeping him down the cellar when the raids was on. She'd to practically have him on her knee, keep him distracted. One time he gets up in the middle of the night, runs outside in just his shirt. We finds him, fetches him back, and after that Ma makes him sleep with her and the girls. Wasn't no good in the end though. One night we're eating dinner and a big 'un goes off nearby and he's off, up the steps and out before Ma can put her plate down. We're all out looking for him, bombs whistling down, but he's gone. Vanished. Nuffink for a couple of days, then Ma hears they found a kid up West in two halves: glass from a shop window done it. She knows it's Spuggy but I don't know how she knows. Keeps a lot of fings to herself, Ma does.'

It's ten past ten when I get to Tooley Street. Ma's looking out for me and it's all right: Rags is out. 'Went at half past eight,' she says. 'Making up for yesterday, I expect.'

'Ask how you were, did he?'

Ma shrugs. 'Yes, he did, in a half-hearted sort of way.' She smiles wanly. 'Didn't make me a cup of tea or anything like that, but I dare say he'll bring me a bottle or two of stout this afternoon, if he can get 'em.'

There aren't many customers. We work like yesterday: Ma serving, me keeping the racks filled up from the back room. It's not exactly hectic and I'm thinking about what Wotsis said: *Keeps a lot of fings to herself, Ma does.* I'm wondering if she heard about a kid buried under the rubble of a bombed-out house, one arm sticking out. All day, every day, whatever else I'm doing I'm thinking about finding that house. What I try to *avoid* thinking about is whether it'll get me home when I do find it. Anyway, the more I think, the likelier it seems that Ma might know where the place is, so when we're having a standup break among the tea-chests, I bring the subject up.

'Ma?'

'What?'

'Wotsis reckons you get to know things: things that happen in the bombing.'

'Aw he *does*, does he? And what sort of *things* is he talking about, eh?'

'Well, like with Spuggy. He'd crossed the river, gone up West, but you found out what happened to him.'

'Spuggy? You know about Spuggy then, do you?'

'Only what guys've told me.'

'Well *guys* should learn to keep their faces shut, if you ask me. I don't want to talk about Spuggy: I *never* talk about him, so it's no use your asking.'

I shake my head. 'It's not about Spuggy, Ma. I was wondering if you heard anything about a kid who was buried under a bombed-out house, with just an arm . . .'

'Spuggy. That's what happened to Spuggy. You said it wasn't about him.'

'It's *not*. I thought Spuggy was cut in—'

'*Before*. Spuggy was buried before he came to us: that's why he couldn't stand being shut in.'

'I didn't know that. The kid I'm talking about . . .'

'*Shoo!* Oi, cat: get out of here, *now!*' I look where Ma's looking, see a ginger moggy rubbing itself against the corner of a chest. A customer must've left the door ajar. Ma runs at it, waving her arms, slopping tea all over, but instead of fleeing back through the shop the cat bounds from chest to chest to the foot of the stairs and up, out of sight.

'Oh *lor*,' goes Ma, 'he *hates* cats, old Rags does. He'll kill it if he finds it here. Kill *me* for letting it in, I wouldn't be surprised.' She looks at me. 'Go after it, Frecks: chase it down. I'd do it myself, but there's the shop.'

I nod. 'No problem, Ma. I'll sort it.' I'm picking my way through the boxes. 'Leave the door wide open: he'll be going like a bullet when he comes down.'

I climb the stairs, hoping the daft animal hasn't burrowed in among the mouldering rags which cover the floor. Take all day to find him if he has. I'm in luck: he's halfway across the room, looking back at me like he's *defying* me to catch him. Careful not to repeat Ma's mistake, I don't charge: in fact I don't go towards him at all, or even look in his direction. Instead I head for the attic stairs with my hands in my pockets, whistling a tune to myself as though I haven't noticed his presence. What I'll do when I reach the foot of the stairs I'm not sure, but at least I'll stop him going up there.

It all goes wrong, of course. Cats're pretty smart: if they *really* want to go somewhere, they'll get there whatever you do. When I reach the stairs, moggy's in the exact spot I first saw him in. Only difference is, he's turned his head and is watching me. What I decide to do is walk slowly towards him, making that daft tch-tch-tch noise everybody makes to cats. I bet when cats get together they imitate us doing that, then fall about laughing. Anyway that's what I do. I figure he'll let me get to a certain point, then turn and run down the stairs.

Well, he does let me get to a certain point, but instead of turning he swerves round me and, without hurrying, trots to the foot of the stairs and up. I can practically hear him saying, *I don't know what you imagined* you *were going to do*.

He doesn't know it and neither do I, but Moggy's about to do his little bit for the war effort.

Forty-Five

They're dangerous, those attic steps. Positively dangerous. They squeak and tremble every time I put a foot down. I don't know what they're fastened to or how, but I feel like it's all going to come away any minute. Ma says Rags sleeps up there: *I* wouldn't. What if a bomb fell nearby?

Anyway the cat's up there and I've promised, so up I go. It's a bit dark at the top and there's a door either side. The one on the left's shut so Moggy must be in the other. There's some light in there – it's coming through a soot-streaked window in the slope of the roof. There's no sign of the cat but there aren't many hiding-places: the room contains only a hard chair, a washstand with basin and ewer and a narrow bed against the wall. Moggy's not under the chair or stand, which leaves the bed. I get down on the bare boards and stick my head under. There's a yowl and the cat streaks past my face. Before I can turn there's a scrabbling sound, a soft thud and a terrific crash. In his panic to escape, Moggy's leapt onto the stand and collided with the basin. Miraculously it's still there, but the ewer's toppled and lies in three pieces on the floor. Needless to say, the cat has vanished.

I pick up the bits of ewer, then put them back. Better let Rags find cat damage than leave proof someone's been in his bedroom, especially since he'd believe it was Ma. I'm dusting myself down when I notice something in the basin. It's a key. Moggy won't have put it there so it must've been under the ewer. Hidden.

I pick it up. It's long, thin and rusty. Nothing in this room locks, so maybe it's the key to the other attic. You can't beat a mysterious key for arousing curiosity. I decide to try it. Maybe I'll find a body: the late Mrs Rags, perhaps.

I leave the bedroom, stick the key in the lock on the other door. It fits and turns so I guessed right about that, though not about the body. It's just a roomful of junk: broken furniture, a bike with a wheel missing, some rolls of mouldy carpet. The skylight's even muckier than the other one. The place pongs a bit but I tiptoe around, seeking whatever it is that makes Rags hide the key. A Welsh dresser stands across the far corner. I peep behind and there it is, squatting on a table made of tea-chests and planks: a box of grey metal with some knobs and a dial. I goggle at the thing with my mouth open and my heart pumping. I may not be the most intelligent guy in the universe but I know a wireless transmitter when I see one, and I'm looking at one now.

Forty-Six

Ma's like, 'What's wrong with that, Frecks? *Lots* of people got the wireless nowadays, keep up with the news. Where's the cat?'

'Not a transmitter, Ma: they have *receivers*, they don't have transmitters. Transmitters're for *sending* wireless messages.'

'All right, so Rags is one of them . . . whatchamacallit . . . wireless fools.'

'Hams.' I shake my head. 'I don't think so, Ma. Why would a wireless ham hide his equipment behind an old dresser in a dark, mucky attic? I bet he's a spy: an enemy agent.'

'Who, old Rags? A *spy*? Don't make me laugh.'

'Why shouldn't he be, Ma? We know they're here in London: why not Rags?'

'Well, for a start he's Jewish. I can't see many Jews falling over theirselves to spy for Hitler, can you? And for another thing he don't *look* like a spy, more like a bookie's runner. *And* he spends all his time in the pub. Who ever heard of a secret agent boozing all day long? Did you *find* the cat, Frecks?'

'No, I didn't find the cat.' She's getting me mad, going on about the flipping cat. 'I don't give a stuff about the *cat*, Ma: that guy's a Nazi. You're *working* for a Nazi. We've got to tell the police.'

'No!' She shakes her head. 'No police, Frecks. Bring *them* sniffing round and we'll all be packed off to ruddy orphanages so fast our feet won't touch.'

'Yeah, but . . . there's a *wireless transmitter* up there, Ma: we can't pretend we haven't seen it, just because we're scared we'll end up in a home. You said yourself there's a war to win.'

'I know.' She's gazing out of the taped-up window, chewing her lip. 'I know, but I think you're mistaken. *Must* be. I mean, don't you see how unlikely it is? It's like one of them pictures you're so fond of. You know: cunning spy outwits police, secret service, everyone; then some kid chasing a cat falls over his wireless and he's caught, just like that. Kid gets medal, spy gets shot. THE END. No.' She shakes her head. 'It's too pat, Frecks. There's an innocent explanation for what you saw up there.'

'So why not tell the police, let Rags give *them* his innocent explanation?'

Ma sighs. 'I *told* you why not. Me and Nell and the others, we haven't lived all these weeks in that cold cellar, eating nothing but spuds and carrots and the broken biscuits Shrapnel lost his life bringing to us, only to turn ourselves in because some picture-mad kid who's been with us about five minutes thinks he's a spy-catcher.'

Ma's voice gets louder and louder as she's saying this: she ends up yelling. I don't want to fall out with Ma – can't afford to – and anyway I know we win the war whether Rags is a spy or not, whether he's *caught* or not, so I hold up my hands like I did the day she came home and found she'd another mouth to feed. 'OK, Ma, you're right. I *am* the new kid on the block and I won't go to the police. I won't tell *anybody*, I promise.'

It's OK. She simmers down, we go on playing at shops. She seems to have forgotten about the cat. I daren't bring my question up again, though, about the bombed-out house, and I can't stop picturing Rags tonight when we've left and the shop's locked up, crouching over his transmitter in the dark attic, sending coded signals to some guy in Berlin.

Forty-Seven

I leave at three, same as yesterday. I'm really down, partly because I haven't managed to ask Ma about the house, partly because I'm fed up feeling hungry all the time and partly because everything looks so shabby. Not to mention every*body*. I've always been mad on World War Two, but I guess that's because I only knew about *bits* of it. I mean, the books and videos *mention* the shortage of grub and clothes, I'm not saying they don't, but it takes like five seconds to mention it: you don't feel what it's *like* to eat nothing but boiled veg day in, day out; to walk the streets in a coat that was made for some tall, fat guy who probably *died* in it. It doesn't tell you how it feels to pee in a pot four guys have peed in or worse already, or to play Snakes and flipping Ladders every night for four hours in the dark while guys fly around dropping bombs on you.

That's not the worst, though. If you've watched or read much about the war, you're bound to have come across some mention of *Dunkirk Spirit*. It's what everybody in Britain is supposed to have been full of during the war: a feeling of all being together in the same boat, having the same job to do, and being determined to pull together with cheery optimism till it was done. I've heard it mentioned loads of times and I've believed in it too, till now. It was hearing yesterday that there are people who'll go through the pockets of the dead to get ration books and other valuable papers that's spoilt it for me. *Their own people*. That's the biggest downer.

Anyway, when Ma gets home just before six she pulls me to one side and hisses, 'I think you might be right after all: tell you later.' I get a feeling things're hotting up.

Forty-Eight

I do the dishes but I don't mention washing-up liquid. We've had sardine sandwiches. Ma saw a queue on her way home and joined it. It's a rule: if you see a queue, join it – if you've got any dosh. In 1940 a queue means there's something worth having. Today it was sardines.

Ma starts wiping. Everybody else is busy. She murmurs, 'His nibs comes in about five, asks has it been quiet, goes upstairs. Half a minute later he's back, looking as if he's about to throttle me. *You went to my room*, he says. *Why?* That ewer couldn't have broken itself, so I start to explain what happened with the cat, except it's *me* chasing it, not you. Well: he comes at me, backs me into a corner, sticks his ugly mug in my face, starts shouting, spit flying out of his mouth. And it ain't about the *cat* – he doesn't seem bothered about that at all – it's 'cause I went upstairs. *You had no right*, he yells, *coming in my room like that. My room is private!* Phew! Good job you put that key back in the washbasin, Frecks: goodness *knows* what he'd have done if he'd thought I'd been in the *other* attic.'

'*Sorry*, I says, *only I* know *you don't like cats: I thought you'd be upset if you come back and found a cat at the top of the house. I'm sure I thought I was doing the best thing, Mr Rags.*'

'*Well, you were not, Sandra*, he says. *You were not doing the best thing, you were doing the worst thing, and if you ever do it again I will dismiss you at once, do you understand?*'

'*Yes sir*, I says. *I'm very sorry, sir, and it won't happen again.*'

'*Then we'll say no more about it*, says he, backing off of me.'

'Wow.' I shake my head. 'Did the guy overreact or what?'

Ma gives me a funny look. 'I don't know that expression, Frecks, but he certainly acted as if he'd something to hide: something more private than an old bed and a ham wireless. I think we ought to watch him.'

'How d'you mean?'

'Spy on him when he goes out: see if he *really* spends all day in the pub.'

I nod. 'Yeah, and at night we could see if he goes in the other attic.'

Ma looks dubious. 'Not easy while the bombing keeps up, Frecks, but we could scout around up there in the daytime if he leaves the key.'

My turn to look dubious. 'I don't think he will, Ma. He's had a scare. Most likely hide it properly this time.'

'Anyway,' she wipes the last teaspoon, spreads the cloth over a chairback, 'I think it's only fair we tell everybody what's happening.' I nod my agreement. We move to join the others.

The siren's gone. Tilley lamps flicker in the draught, illuminating tables which have been set up as usual for Ludo, Snakes and Ladders. Everybody's waiting for us. Everything looks the same but it's not. Victory Hall stands poised to do its bit for victory.

Forty-Nine

'So you fink he's a *real* spy?' breathes Mouse, when Ma's told her story.

Ma pulls a face. 'I dunno, Mouse: all I know is, he's got a wireless transmitter and he acts like a man with a secret. It's up to us to find out if he's a spy or not.'

'Us?' Siren's eyes light up. 'You mean we can *all* play?'

''Tain't *playing*, Siren, it's serious. And yes, everybody's part of my plan.'

I look at her. 'You've got a plan?'

''Course.' *Keeps a lot of fings to herself, Ma does.*

'Tell us then,' goes Bertie.

'I *am*,' snaps Ma, 'if you give us a chance.'

Everybody's eyes are on her face. Nobody speaks.

'What we need to know,' she begins, 'is two things. One: what does old Rags get up to all day when he's not in the shop? And two: is there anything to be found in the shop which might prove he's a spy? Besides the transmitter, I mean.'

'Ain't the transmitter *enough*?' asks Bertie.

Ma shakes her head. 'No, 'cause there's wireless hams. We'd look daft, wouldn't we, telling the police we've caught a spy and he turns out to be a wireless ham? So: how do we find out the answer to number one? We shadow him, that's how.'

Nell frowns. 'What's *shadow*, Ma?'

'Means follow, Nell. We follow him, without him knowing he's being followed. T'ain't easy: private detectives do it, but they're trained. D'you think *you* could manage it?'

''Course.'

'Good, because you'll lead Number One Commando.'

'Eh? Come again.'

'Number One Commando: Wotsis, Mouse, you. You lead. Bertie?'

'What?'

'Number Two Commando: Siren and you.'

'Who leads?'

'You're the same age: *both* lead.'

'So what do we *do*, us commandos?'

'I told you, Bertie: you *shadow*. In turns: day on, day off. Very responsible job, could be dangerous.'

Wotsis grins. 'Wizard. What about you and Frecks, Ma?'

Ma smiles. 'We're in the shop already: we'll start combing the place for evidence, top to bottom.'

'When do we start?' asks Mouse.

'Tomorrow, except Two Commando: they'll do morning jobs tomorrow, shadow on Thursday.'

'Morning *jobs*?' goes Bertie, looking sick as a parrot.

Ma nods. 'Certainly: even commandos keep their billets spick and span, you know, and you'll have Frecks to help you.' She stands up, grins round at us all.

'Make a change from Snakes and Ladders, won't it?'

Fifty

So when Ma leaves for work next morning, Nell, Wotsis and Mouse head for Tooley Street too. They don't walk *with* her, they practise shadowing her. Ma's idea. 'I'll keep looking behind,' she warns, 'and you better not look interested or I'll shoot you dead with this.' She sticks out two fingers as a gun.

I help Bertie and Siren with the jobs. Bertie knows where to take the chamber-pots, and I go alone for water. Three trips. Shrapnel's sign is still on the door. DANGER – UNEXPLODED BOMB. Makes me sad.

When I'm staggering along the street for the third time with a sloshing bucket in each hand, two women start to catch up with me. I can hear them giggling, making remarks. As they draw level, one says, 'What's *that* for, dearie?'

'Well,' I tell her, 'some people wash in it, or you can drink it, or if you like you can stick your head in it and *drown* your flipping self.'

She doesn't like it. Her mouth drops open and she goes, 'Oh!' plucking at her friend's sleeve. 'Did you *hear* what he said to me, cheeky young blighter?' As they overtake she snarls, 'Running wild, kids today. Never ought to have shut the schools.'

'Shame they didn't shut your gob while they were at it,' I retort. She lets out a little shriek and they both break into a trot and disappear round a corner. I'm laughing so much I spill more water than usual. Lippy kids must be rare in 1940.

I join Ma just after ten. She shows me where One Commando loitered till Rags left the shop, then followed him, playing tag and looking in shop windows all the way. 'I hope they'll be OK,' I murmur.

''*Course* they will,' says Ma. 'D'you think I'd let 'em *do* it, otherwise?' She smiles. 'If he notices they're following him he'll only think they're a bunch of urchins trying to amuse theirselves till schools open again.'

As I expected, both attics are locked now. 'He'll have the key on him,' I tell Ma.

She nods. 'Yes, I expect so. We'll just have to search the shop, the back room and the big one upstairs, see if anything turns up. D'you want to make a start?'

'Sure.'

'Better not be rummaging about in here when there's a customer, Frecks: keep an eye on the door, will you?'

As it happens a customer comes in right then, so I vanish through the bead curtain. Short of emptying all the chests and cases, which I'm not going to do, there's hardly anywhere to search in the back room. There's just a cupboard under the sink with a sliding door, and I carry out a thorough inspection of its greasy, webby interior without finding anything of interest, unless you're interested in woodlice and spider eggs. After that I rinse my hands and mooch about kicking stuff till the customer leaves and I can go through to the shop.

Ma looks up. 'Anything?'

'Naw. What did she buy?'

'That turquoise dress with the sequins off the shilling rack.'

'She *didn't*.'

'She did.'

'Did she *say* she wanted to look like a ninety-year-old mermaid that's been attacked by sharks?'

'*Frecks!* You're awful.'

'Well, I can't understand what anybody'd *do* with a rag like that. Better wearing a bin-bag.'

'A what?'

'A . . . bean bag.'

'You're daft as well as awful. Look in these drawers while we're free.'

There's a line of seven drawers under the counter. They turn out to be full of buttons, buckles, hatpins, shoelaces, strips of elastic: stuff that's dropped off the good-as-new apparel for the discerning. I shove my polluted hand to the back of the seventh, which looks just like the other six and bingo! my fingers hit something hard that jingles. I grab whatever it is and pull it out, and I'm looking at a *ginormous* keyring with every sort of key you can think of. The flat brass ones are dull, the long iron ones rusty. The only shine is on a shoal of tiny chrome-plated ones which probably came with suitcases in the remote past.

'Ma?' I hold up the bunch, rattle it. It's really heavy.

She peers, comes over. 'What you got?'

'Keys, loads of 'em. Some sad geezer's key collection. What's the chances . . .

'. . . of one of 'em fitting the attic?' she finishes. 'Depends, dunnit? If old Rags found it in a pocket or something, it'll have nothing to do with this place. But if the keys've been put on one by one over the years, *here*, some might be spares for locks here. It's worth a try, innit?'

It was.

Fifty-One

Climbing the shaky stairs I picture myself trying key after key, first in one lock then the other. It doesn't happen like that. I decide to try the longest one first, on the junk-room door, and it slips in and turns dead easy. I can't believe it. I suppose it looks like the key I found in the basin and I've remembered subconsciously: that's the logical explanation. Anyway I twist the knob and the door creaks open and I'm in.

Everything's the same. I go straight across to the Welsh dresser, thinking maybe Rags'll have moved the transmitter but he hasn't. I sit down on the crate he uses for a chair and search the plank table. The dresser makes it very dark so it's a matter of feeling around. Rags must carry a torch or something when he uses the transmitter at night: there's no electric light up here. Talking of Rags, it feels decidedly spooky being in his secret domain like this: I'm straining my ears for creaks on the stair, knowing he could show up any minute. If I'm to spend time up here in future, Ma and I will have to work out some way she can warn me if he comes back unexpectedly.

There's nothing on the table. I push the crate aside, kneel down and start patting the floor. I've no clear idea what I hope to find: a code book perhaps, or something written in German. Anyway there's nothing. I get up and sit down on the crate for a think. *If I was an enemy agent, where would I put documents and stuff? There must be documents, surely: where would I hide 'em? Dresser? Rolls of carpet?*

I should look in these places, but I'm getting more and more jumpy. I decide to go down, give Ma the good news about the key and arrange some sort of warning signal with her. Then I'll come back and search properly. I relock the door, then on impulse try the same key in the one opposite. To my amazement it works. I lock it again and tiptoe gingerly down, grinning like the Cheshire cat.

Fifty-Two

'Bingo!'

'You what?'

'Er . . . jingo.' I rattle the bunch, holding the one that counts. 'See this?'

''Course: I'm not blind.'

'Opens both attics.'

'Never.'

'Does though, I've tried it.'

'Our lucky day. Find anything?'

'Not yet: something to see to first.' I tell her we need a signal: a warning for if Rags comes back early.

'He's never come back early while I've worked here.'

'There's always a first time. I feel jumpy just *being* here, let alone rooting through his stuff.'

'Being here's not hard: if he turns up you're a customer. I agree we need a plan for if he comes while you're upstairs. What can we do?'

We rack our brains. Two customers come in while we're thinking, which counts as a mad rush in *this* shop. I go through the curtain. *Pity there's no mobile phones in 1940, that'd solve it.*

When I come out Ma says, 'I've got it.'

'Wizard, how does it go?'

'It'll only work if you leave the door open up there.'

'I always do.'

'Good, then this is what we do. He comes in, asks if it's been quiet. I say yes, same as always. If he's brought a bottle for me he plonks it on the counter and gives me a wink. Then he goes through the curtain and across to the stairs. I follow, calling after him that I forgot to show him something important. I make it loud enough for you to hear. He stops, I show him this important thing that's not important at all really, and by the time he's *told* me it's not, you've concealed yourself, as it says in detective stories.'

'Brilliant.' I grin, then frown. 'What will you show him though?'

'This.' She fishes in her pinny pocket, brings out a fancy cigarette case. 'I found it in a suit some geezer swopped the other day. It looks like gold but it isn't. I'll pretend to think it is.'

'You're a genius.'

She shakes her curls. 'Wouldn't be working here if I was. Where'll you hide?'

I smile. 'There's six rolls of stinky old carpet in the junk room: I'll take my pick.'

'It's you that's a genius, Frecks.'

'That's right, Ma: the Einstein of Bermondsey.'

'Einstein's German.'

'But not Nazi: you can't be a Nazi if there's evidence of a brain.'

We laugh, then I go through and put the kettle on.

Fifty-Three

We drink some sugarless tea, then I go back up. It feels comfier now we've got the signal. I've got a box of matches too, and a bit of candle. Everybody keeps candles in case of power-cuts. I unlock the junk-room door, leave it open and light my candle. By its light I choose the carpet I'll hide in if I have to. I unroll it, lie down, pull one end over my body and roll. It smells of toadstools and I've no way of knowing what it looks like with me inside: I have to hope it'll be good enough in the gloom.

I do another search behind the dresser. I can actually see now but the result's the same. There's nothing. I try the dresser drawers but they're empty. After some fruitless rummaging among the rest of the junk, I abandon the place and let myself into Rags's bedroom.

He's taken the bits of jug away but the basin's still on the stand. Needless to say there's no key in it. There's hardly anywhere to search in this bare room, but I get down and look under the bed. It's not romantic, even by candlelight. Dust-bunnies. One trodden-down carpet slipper. A chamber-pot, cracked. Rags may be a spy but he's no housekeeper, nothing's disturbed this dust except the cat.

I'm about to get up off my knees when something catches my eye. Between the mesh of the bedsprings and the mattress is a square of paper. I back up, lift the mattress and take out the paper. It's folded a couple of times and has a diamond pattern embossed on one side from the mesh. I stick the candle to the floor with a blob of wax, unfold the paper and smooth it on the boards so the light falls across it.

It's a map. A map of Bermondsey. 'Edition of 1916' it says at the top. Streets and houses and railway lines. The Thames, with Tower Bridge and London Bridge. And bleeding off the right-hand edge is the park where Cheese Roll and the others man their light. Even the bandstand's marked. It's a black-and-white map, but scattered across it are red circles someone's drawn with a wax pencil. Some are just circles, others have crosses in them, like hot cross buns.

My heart's thumping. *This is it*, I tell myself. *Evidence. Proof. Why would a wireless ham have this map? Why would he hide it under his mattress?* Rapidly I refold the map, blow out the candle, get to my feet. *Show Ma quick, then put it back exactly as it was. Bummer no one's invented the photocopier yet. Mobile phone, copier. Hey: why don't I invent them, make a fortune?*

Fifty-Four

We spread it on the floor behind the counter and I watch the door while Ma has what she calls a dekko. I can tell she's impressed with my find. She's kneeling forward with her nose practically touching the paper, peering at the red rings and the words in minute print they partly obscure. When a customer comes in she gets up, pretends she's looking for something under the counter. The woman browses the rails but leaves empty-handed, so they're not all suckers. The second she's gone Ma's down again, poring.

She's at it for about half an hour. I'm on tenterhooks the whole time in case Rags shows up. *Oh hi, Mr Rags, you remember me: I brought you that message from Sandra. I was just passing and I thought I'd pop in and go through your personal stuff. You know: your slipper, your bedding, that wireless transmitter and this map. You'll never guess where I found the map, by the way: only under your mattress, that's all. I bet you've been looking everywhere for it, haven't you?* Come on, Ma, for Pete's sake.

She gets up frowning, folding the map. 'Rings've got *me* flummoxed, Frecks: I hoped they'd turn out to be factories or military sites or something but they're not. They're all over. And I don't understand why some of 'em got crosses and some ain't.' She pulls a face. 'Maybe the geezer's a wireless ham after all.'

'No way,' I shake my head. 'Not when he has to hide stuff under his mattress. It'll be interesting to see where he's taken One Commando today.'

'Yes, unless it turns out they've spent six hours gawping at the outside of a pub.'

I take the map upstairs and put it back exactly where I found it. I even line up the marks with the bedspring. I lift the blob of wax off the floorboard with my fingernail, like picking a scab, and drop it in my pocket. I've got the candle again and I have a really careful look round to make sure I won't be leaving any trace of my visit. I find I'm not sure exactly how the blanket hung, but decide he's not likely to remember either. I leave, locking the door. Before going downstairs I find a sliver of wood among the dust and splinters on the floor and slip it into the crack between the junk-room door and its jamb. Rags won't spot it, but if he opens the door tonight the sliver'll fall and I'll know tomorrow he's been in there. Nothing much, I'll admit, but when you're spying on a spy every little helps.

Fifty-Five

I get back to Victory Hall and find Two Commando has had a washday. A line stretches right across the cellar with everybody's underwear dangling from it. It's been washed in cold water with bits of hard soap, so it's not exactly a snowy-white scene. It's a swine getting stuff dry when you can't hang out and there's no fire, but Bertie tells me Ma insists on everybody having a change of underclothes fortnightly. She's bought most of the items from Rags, and rags is what they are but they're clean rags, or at any rate as clean as most people's stuff in the Blitz. It says a lot about what a together person Ma is that she can be bothered, in the middle of all the hassle we cause her, to see we keep ourselves decent.

One Commando comes in at half-five. Nell says Rags never spotted them and that he's definitely up to something, but they're not saying anything else till Ma gets back. We light Aladdin and start getting dinner ready, ducking under the clothes-line every time we move.

Ma crawls underground just in time for the sirens. She's had a drop of stout so we creep about giving her space till she's ready for us. We're having vegetable stew with dumplings. When it's ready, Nell goes through and fetches Ma and we all sit down to eat.

Ma spoons a hunk of soggy dumpling into her mouth and chews thoughtfully. Everybody's watching her. She knows this and makes us wait: it's a game she plays. When a slow smile starts to creep across her face we begin to relax. Finally she swallows, nods and says, 'Good dumpling, Siren,' and everybody laughs.

'All right.' Ma looks at Nell. 'Where did One Commando get to and what did Rags do?'

'I've got it all down here, Ma.' Nell produces a small notebook and consults it. 'We shadowed him across London Bridge, Ma, and he went in a pub called the Bricklayer's Arms. He was in there ages. We hung about, looking in windows and that. Thought he was there for the duration. Half-ten he comes out and we follow. He walks a bit, seems to be looking for sumfink. Suddenly he stops. Nuffink special that we can see, just one of them whatsits – street shelters. He looks at it for a bit, walks right round it, moves away. We're coming along behind him on the ovver side. After a bit he fishes sumfink out of his coat, notebook or sumfink, writes in it with a bit of a pencil wivvout stopping, puts it away and walks on till he comes to anovver pub, the Monkey. Goes in. We all groan, we know it's more hanging about. Me and Mouse goes off to find a lavatory and a drink of water, leaving Wotsis on sentry duty. When we get back the geezer's still inside so Wotsis nips off. Minute he's out of sight, here comes Rags. All I can do is follow by myself, leave Mouse to tell Wotsis which way I went.'

Ma looks at Mouse. 'Weren't you scared, Mouse, all by yourself?'

'No.' You can hear the indignation in his voice. 'I wasn't scared at all. I kept calm, watched Nell out of sight, then waited. It wasn't that long.'

Ma smiles. 'You were brave, Mouse: a hero.' She spears a cube of swede, puts it in her mouth, turns to Nell. 'So where did he take you?'

Nell looks in the notebook, shrugs. 'Some railway arches, I fink: he seemed interested in them. Stood looking, went under one, looked up.' She grins. 'I half expected him to shout. You know: for the echo, but he didn't. He moved on. I was worried about Mouse and Wotsis but I had to follow. A few yards, and out come the book and pencil again. Writes on the move, like before. While he's writing I look back and see the ovvers in the distance. Two minutes and we're togevver again, opposite the Old London Bridge.'

'Another pub?'

'Yes.'

'And after that?'

Nell shakes her head. 'Nuffink, Ma. He's ages in the pub, and when he comes out he sets off back the way he come. We shadow a bit to make sure, then break off and start making our way home.'

'Thank you, Nell. I call that a professional job, taking notes and everything. Well done, One Commando.'

Nell, Mouse and Wotsis grin and glow. I look at Ma. 'What about *Rags's* notes though: what d'you reckon *they're* in aid of?'

Ma looks solemn. 'I'm starting to have my suspicions, Frecks, but I hope they're wrong 'cause they're nasty. I need another dekko at the map you found.' She nods towards the clothes-line. 'No need to ask how Two Commando performed. Well done, you two.'

That's Ma. Whatever's happening, however much she's got on her plate she remembers everybody. Their *feelings*. Where would her ragtag little army be without her?

Fifty-Six

When I get to the shop Thursday morning, she's been up already and got the map. Yesterday we took the attic key off the ring and hid it in the back room. One thing about Rags's: plenty of places to hide stuff. The rest of the bunch is back in drawer seven.

'Come here, Frecks,' she says as I'm hanging my coat up. 'I want to show you something.' The map's open on the counter. I glance nervously towards the door. ''S OK,' she says. Bertie or Siren'll warn us if he looks to be coming back early.' Thinks of everything, Ma.

'What you got?' I lean in and she stabs the map with her finger.

'See what that is?'

'Yeah: red circle with a cross.'

'Not *that*, you twerp: what's he *drawn* it on, and if you say a flippin' map you'll get a poke in the eye.'

It isn't easy to make out what the circle's covering – not in this light. I squint at the diagram. 'Looks like a viaduct, Ma. Railway viaduct.' As I say these words it comes to me what I'm looking at. 'It's the Stainer Street arch, where . . .'

'That's right, Frecks. He's circled the Stainer Street arch and put a cross through the circle. Now why the cross, d'you think?'

'A lot of 'em have crosses, Ma.'

'I know, and a lot don't. Look.' She points to a plain circle. 'That's St Patrick's church and school, just across the river. No cross. What's the difference between St Patrick's and that arch, Frecks? Think about it.'

I think. *There's loads of differences. One's a church, one's a viaduct. One's north of the river, one's south. One got bombed, the other didn't.* The last one's the only one that isn't too obvious to mention, so I mention it. 'Arch was bombed, church wasn't.'

'Correct, except I think you should have said *yet*: the church isn't bombed *yet.*'

'What d'you mean, Ma?'

She straightens up, looks at me. 'I've found five places I know under open circles, Frecks, and three under crosses. The five under open circles haven't been bombed, but all three with crosses have, including Stainer Street. What does that tell us?' I'm not quite with her, but that's OK because she doesn't wait for my answer. 'It tells us Rags draws rings round places that're *going* to be bombed, then crosses 'em through when they *have* been.'

'But how does he know . . .'

''Cause *he's* the one who's telling the bombers where to bomb, Frecks. *Must* be.'

I stare at her. It sounds ridiculous what she's saying. Impossible. Of course, she doesn't know what old Hitler and his mates're busy doing to Rags's own people right now and I *do*, and I just can't get my head round the idea of a Jewish guy guiding Nazi planes. It's crazy. When I speak my voice is a croak. 'What does he do, then? Stand in one of his circles with a torch, flashing it at the sky? He'd be blown to smithereens.'

Ma shakes her head. 'I dunno, Frecks, I'm not up in these things. Maybe he does it with his wireless but one thing's definite: he's *something* to do with the bombing.'

I swallow, nod. 'Seems like it, Ma. What you gonna do?'

She curls her hands into fists on the counter. 'I know what I'd *like* to do. I'd like to wait till he puts my bottle of stout on this counter and turns his back, then pick it up and smash it against his skull again and again till he's dead.' Her eyes fill with tears.

'He killed Shrapnel, Frecks. I'm working for the man who killed Shrapnel.' She yanks a hanky from her pinny and starts boo-hooing into it, her shoulders shaking.

I desperately wish I could help her but I don't know what to do. I lay a hand on her shoulder and croak, 'It's OK, Ma, he'll pay. They'll *all* pay. They don't know what bombing *is* but they're going to find out, by golly they are. Give it three years.'

I know it's stupid of me to say these words – stupid and dangerous – but I can't stop myself. It's seeing her in so much pain after all she's done for me. For us. Afterwards I find myself hoping she was too upset at the time to take in what I said, and I'm relieved when she doesn't mention it again.

She doesn't mention it, but that doesn't mean she hasn't taken it in. Not a lot gets past old Ma.

Fifty-Seven

Two Commando's report shows that Rags has done pretty much the same as yesterday, except that he's stayed south of the river. When Bertie remarks that the guy seems interested in shelters and churches Ma nods, but doesn't say anything. She's decided not to share her terrible suspicion with the others till there's no possibility she could be wrong. She dreads the prospect, but she'll go on working for Rags till events put his guilt beyond doubt.

And that's how it goes for the next few days: One and Two Commandos taking turns at shadowing. Ma minding the shop, me searching. Rags visits Stainer Street Friday morning, stands gazing at the devastation while One Commando gazes at *him*. The dead have been removed, of course: Ma hasn't been able to find out what the authorities have done with the unidentified. His visit goes in Nell's notebook, but only Ma and I know its significance.

The bombers keep coming, night after night. I sit over a Snakes and Ladders board listening to their engines' drone. Back (*forward?*) in Witchfield I'd imagined myself enthralled in this situation, wondering if I was hearing Heinkels, Junkers, Dorniers. In fact I thought I'd be outside braving the bombs, gazing into the sky. Now I have the opportunity I find I don't care. Far from conjuring up images of Heinkels, Junkers or Dorniers, the engine noise makes me see rows of humps under bloody sheets, a kid called Spuggy sliced in two. And when the sky's silent for a while I think yearningly about hot pepperoni pizza with three sorts of cheese and a heap of fries on the side. Or worse, I think about my mum and wonder if she's thinking about *me*. I'm hungry, bored and scared, and I want to go home.

Fifty-Eight

Thursday 17 October 1940. An eventful day to say the least, and one I'll never forget. One Commando is shadowing. They don't know it yet but Rags will spot them today. In fact he'll spot them at exactly the same time as me and Ma borrow the map from under his mattress for the last time and decide enough's enough. Ma will tell the kids, I'll slope off and tell somebody else, and all hell will break loose.

But I'm getting ahead of myself. I want to tell about Rags and One Commando first. This is what happened, though in a way it was to be a long, long time before I'd find out about it.

Nell, Wotsis and Mouse shadow Ma north to Tooley Street again. She's stopped trying to catch them at it: the game's worn a bit thin, and anyway the whole thing feels less like a game now. Rags leaves the shop as usual, and One Commando follows. What none of us knows is that Rags has become suspicious – not of One Commando, but of Ma. This is partly my fault. I've grown careless while ferreting about in the attics, and Rags has noticed little changes in the position of a crate, the lie of a blanket, which causes him to suspect Ma of going up there in his absence. Probably the only reason he hasn't challenged her about it is that he keeps both rooms locked and can't understand how his assistant is getting in.

Anyway he's jumpy, and more watchful than usual, and around lunchtime he comes out of a pub and spots three kids across the way. They're playing: two twirling a rope for the other to skip, but something about them makes him uneasy. He's sure he's seen them before, in another borough. He walks on, finding ways of glancing back without making it obvious, and yes, they're definitely following him. They're a ragged bunch too – their parents obviously don't know how to dress a child properly. Look at the *girl*: what sort of mother sends her child out to play wearing a straw hat decorated with cherries? As Rags asks himself this, he remembers having had one similar in the shop. This causes him to pay close attention to the trio's clothes, and he soon realises they include garments young Sandra has paid him coppers for recently. He's assumed she wanted them for younger brothers and sisters, but these three don't look like siblings.

He's seriously worried. But for the clothes, he might dismiss the incident as bored kids following him as a game, but some of the garments form a link to Sandra, and he's found cause to be distrustful of her already. What if she's set these urchins to spy on him? It sounds unlikely, but a man in his situation can't be too careful. He decides to give them the slip, then follow *them*. Who knows? Perhaps they'll lead him to their boss.

Fifty-Nine

When we meet in Victory Hall at the end of the day, we know nothing of this. What we *do* know – what me and Ma know anyway – is that more circles have been appearing on Rags's map every night, and more crosses, and that enough is enough.

'Look, everybody.' Ma unfolds the map and smooths it on the table. 'We've pinched it because it doesn't matter now if its owner finds it gone: neither of us will ever be in Rags's shop again. Bombs or no bombs, we take our evidence to the police tonight. Among that evidence will be Nell's and Bertie's notebooks. Every structure Rags has shown an interest in while being shadowed has been circled on his map. Some of them are rubble already, which is why we won't wait a day longer.'

As the kids lean in, Ma shows them the entries in the notebooks and the corresponding rings on the map. 'Apart from three – a tannery, a button factory and a searchlight battery – they're all public shelters, viaducts, schools and church halls.'

'Why?' asks Siren. 'Why would a spy bother with places like that when there's docks and war factories? You'd think Hitler'd want *them* bombed, not schools and churches: they're all empty anyway.'

Ma nods. 'That's what Frecks and me asked ourselves, Siren; then it dawned on us.' She looks round the circle of expectant faces. I've sort of switched off at this point because of something Ma said a minute ago. *Apart from three – a tannery, a button factory and a searchlight battery*. A searchlight battery. I'm contorting my neck trying to see where the searchlight battery is because the map's sideways from where I'm standing.

'You see,' continues Ma, 'these schools and church halls *aren't* empty. Every one of them is in use as a rest centre. Every one of them is packed with bombed-out families. And at night the shelters are packed as well, and the arches.'

Mouse swallows. 'You mean . . . you fink Rags goes round seeing where there's loads of people at night, then tells the bombers?'

'That's exactly what I think, Mouse.' She sighs. 'I don't *want* to think it – it's horrid – but Frecks and I have talked about it and it seems to be the only explanation that fits the stuff in the notebooks and the circles on the map. And it makes sense in a nasty sort of way.'

Nell looks at her. 'What sort of way, Ma?'

'Well . . .' She thinks a bit, then says, 'Why d'you think the King and Queen visit streets that've been bombed the night before, Nell?'

'To see for theirselves, I suppose.'

Ma nods. 'That's part of it but there's another reason: a more important one.'

I'm sort of half-following this conversation. 'I think I know,' I volunteer. I do know because I've read about it on the Internet but of course I can't say that. 'Civilian morale.'

'Cor!' scoffs Wotsis. 'Frecks has swallowed a bleat'n *dictionary*.'

Ma smiles. 'You're probably right, Wotsis, but so's Frecks. The King and Queen walk round to show themselves to the people to remind 'em that they're sharing the danger every night in Buckingham Palace. They're saying, *Look: we're in London too, we haven't run away*. It bucks people up and that's called morale.'

'Yes.' I know I shouldn't but I can't resist chipping in. 'That's why people who used to shout rude words at them stopped after the Palace itself was bombed: it proved *they* could be bombed out too. Killed, even.' I could've added that in fact the royals aren't in Buckingham Palace at night but out at Sandringham, but that's not revealed till long after the war and I'm in enough hassle as it is.

The kids're looking a bit green about the gills as the nature of Rags's deed sinks in, and Ma's asking them to imagine what it does to civilian morale when a rest centre is hit and hundreds of people are blown to bits. 'It's worse than losing a battleship,' she says.

I ease myself out of the circle and slink towards the steps, hoping nobody'll notice. I feel bad about running out on Ma in her hour of need but I can't help it: there's something I have to do.

Sixty

I don't know exactly what Rags does after he spots One Commando shadowing him, but it must go something like this. He hurries on till Nell and the others are unsighted for a moment – maybe there's a bend. He ducks into an alleyway. The kids come round the bend expecting to see him in front of them but there's no sign of him. He can't have reached the next bend, it's too far. They search but he's crafty, stays one move ahead all the time. After a bit they realise they aren't going to pick up his trail again so they do the only thing they can do: turn for home. They've no way of knowing Rags is shadowing *them* now.

They lead him straight to the ruined pub. To Victory Hall. He must be amazed when they get down on their knees one by one, crawl under an old chair and vanish. It takes him a minute to work out what's happening, but he does. Pubs have cellars, it's where the beer is kept. So, three kids are using the cellar of the Victory as a den. Three kids who are wearing clothes from his shop, and who have been following him. He hangs about for a while to see if they'll come out, but they don't. Maybe they're *living* in the cellar: perhaps this is their home.

Three kids, wearing clothes purchased in his shop by his employee Sandra, living in a cellar, following him around. Why would Sandra buy clothes for three homeless urchins? *Because she's a homeless urchin herself.* She says she lives with her mum, has mentioned sisters and brothers, but how does he know really? She just walked into the shop one morning, said she needed work. She'd no identity card: claimed she'd forgotten it, would bring it in tomorrow without fail. She never did, and after reminding her a couple of times he let it go. She was a good worker who seemed content with the paltry sum he gave her at the end of each day, plus a bottle or two of stout. The arrangement suited them both.

Now he thinks, *I was careless: I knew nothing about the girl, yet I gave her the run of the place. Left her unsupervised for hours at a time. I didn't even lock the attic, fool that I am. There was nothing to stop her exploring. Nothing at all. Suppose . . . suppose she's seen the transmitter, knows what it is? She'd want to go rummaging about then, wouldn't she? That would explain why my things have been disturbed. Perhaps the adventure with the cat was not her first climb to the top of the house. Perhaps there never was a cat.*

A *second* key?

More than half convinced Ma's onto him, he rushes back to the shop. He's got a plan, which is to follow the girl when she leaves work. If she goes to the bombed-out pub, it'll prove she's in league with those three kids. It'll mean that she put them up to following him, that they know what he's doing.

It'll mean they must die.

Sixty-One

I haven't brought my coat and it's a cold evening. The sirens have sounded, which means I'm not supposed to be wandering about: I'm keeping my eyes skinned for air-raid wardens and police.

In case you haven't guessed, I'm off to the park. That murdering so-and-so Rags has drawn one of his red circles right where Cheese Roll and his mates have their searchlight, which means he's directed the Luftwaffe to pay them a special visit. Not *bound* to be tonight, but could be. They've been good to me, I've got to warn them. Luckily, the bombers aren't overhead yet.

It's weird, moving through a city with no lights and nobody about. Like a ghost-town. I avoid the main road, hurrying through little streets of terraced houses whose occupants will be huddled in Morrison shelters in the celler, or locked up and gone to the nearest public shelter. They have to lock up because of looters. It's rotten, but there are geezers who sneak about when there's a raid on, trying doors, nicking people's stuff while they're away. I'm extra nervous because I could easily be taken for one of them, and some members of the Home Guard have sworn they'll shoot looters on sight. If this was 2002 instead of 1940 the tabloids'd probably call it the *Shootaloota Pledge*.

I reach the park without being challenged. It's pitch dark among the trees, but at least there won't be wardens. Still no bombers so the searchlight's switched off, leaving me to find the battery by feel.

Using the bandstand as a guide I find the right path and follow it through drifts of fallen leaves till the trees thin and I'm standing at the edge of the open space. The light in its horseshoe of sandbags is just a darker hump in the dark, but someone's moving about out there with a dimmed-down torch and voices murmur. As I stand peering through the gloom I hear the distant throb of aero engines and an ack-ack battery somewhere opens up. Any second now the guys'll switch on, revealing their position to the planes Rags has sent to obliterate them. Without thinking I start forward with a cry of 'Wait: don't switch on!'

What a plonker. I haven't taken four steps when a voice barks, 'Halt, who goes?'

I stop dead. A figure looms. Guy with a rifle, pointed straight at me. I put my hands up like some prat in a movie, except in movies no one pees in his pants. My heart's kicking me so hard in the ribs I think I'll pass out. 'F-friend,' I manage to bleat.

The light comes on. Guy sees I'm a kid, swears, lowers his weapon. 'What the bleat'n'ell d'you think you're *playing* at, laddie?' I recognise him, it's Redhead. 'I damn near *shot* you, you little basket.'

'I . . . I know. Sorry. I came with a message for Cheese . . . for the corporal.'

'*Message?*' He's mad: totally ape-shape.

I nod miserably, hoping he won't notice my trousers.

'Yes, it's urgent. You're going to be bombed. There's this spy . . .'

The noise swells as aircraft approach and nearby batteries start firing. The finger of light swings across the sky, feeling for the intruder. These guys're busy, no time to mess with me. I feel a total prat. Redhead snarls something, grabs my arm, starts lugging me across the grass. The din is tearing up the night, the ground trembling. I'm dizzy, losing my balance. Redhead drags me to the sandbags, throws me down. There's a hellish clattering, a flat bang.

The light's gone out.

Sixty-Two

It'll mean they must die.

Unbeknown to me or the friends I've left behind at Victory Hall, Rags has had all of his suspicions confirmed. Shadowing Ma through teatime twilit streets, he's watched her mount the heap of rubble of what was once a pub and crawl under the chair which camouflages the entrance to its cellar. He now knows for certain that his assistant is connected to the trio of urchins he followed here earlier. They're in league, and they're onto him.

Feeling reasonably confident that none of them will leave the cellar once the sirens have wailed, he leaves the doorway he's been lurking in and strides northwest towards Tooley Street. There's something in the shop he's going to need. It lies wrapped in a oily rag under a loose floorboard in his bedroom. He's never used it but is perfectly prepared to do so if necessary, and it is necessary now.

He lets himself into the shop just as the first wave of bombers approaches the city. Preferring not to be at the top of the house when the raid begins, he takes the rickety steps two at a time. He's not in a panic but he's certainly frightened and this is understandable, since a few words from the girl or one of her urchins is all it would take to put him in front of a firing squad. He kneels groping for the loose board. With the snub-nosed automatic heavy in his hand he feels better. Those lethal words will never be spoken: he *is* a firing squad.

The trickiest part of murder is getting rid of the body. Or bodies. Rags isn't worried though: he's got the perfect method at his fingertips. All it will take is one more ring on the map, a simple navigational calculation and a brief coded transmission and *boom!* Twenty-four hours from now the cellar and its grisly contents will be blown to atoms. The children will simply have disappeared, like countless thousands of others all over Europe.

C'est la guerre.

Sixty-Three

The light's gone out.

I'm lying on wet grass with one cheek pressed against the rough hardness of sandbags. Through the infernal din which seems to fill the world comes the sound of someone screaming. Men are moving to and fro urgently, panting and cursing. I feel and hear them, I do not see. Somebody nearby must be speaking into a radio: *Parka Ranger to Flashlight . . . come in, Flashlight. Parka Ranger to . . .*

Bogger fired straight down our beam. I recognise Cheese Roll's voice, know what he must be talking about. Sometimes, when a bomber was caught in the beam of a searchlight so that ack-ack batteries could concentrate their fire on it, an air-gunner would fire his machine-guns into the blinding glare in the hope of shooting out the light. It didn't often work, because a searchlight is a tiny target and the gunner is shooting blind from a moving platform, but now and then it did. This is what must've happened to the corporal's light.

The wave of planes goes over, the engine noise recedes. One by one the guns cease firing. It's easier to hear the screaming now, and other voices too. I hear: 'What's taking 'em so bleat'n long?' and, 'Why no morphine in first-aid kits, what use is a soddin' *eye*-bath?' A part of me wants to offer help, but I'd probably only get in the way and I've done enough of that already. I ease myself into a sitting position but that's all. I avoid looking towards the screams.

A vehicle approaches and stops, its engine running. ''Bout bleat'n time,' says someone, Redhead I think. Feet thud on turf, a hooded light dances about, there are murmurs. The screaming drops to a whimper, which fades to nothing. Somebody sighs with relief. The searchlights are going out, one by one. I hear them carry the casualty to the ambulance, which moves off. The guys feel better now their mate's in good hands, you can tell. One even laughs.

I notice I'm chilled to the bone. Better get up, warn the corporal, get back. I'm about to shift myself when somebody comes and looks down at me. 'Now,' grunts Cheese Roll, 'you'd better explain to me what the heck you think you're doing wandering about in the middle of a raid, nearly getting yourself shot by my sentry and generally making a darned nuisance of yourself.'

'There's this German spy,' I blurt. It sounds like a load of cobblers, even to me.

Sixty-Four

Rags gets back to his doorway across the road from Victory Hall as the sound of aero engines recedes. He's jumpy: this lull in the bombardment is bound to bring wardens and others onto the streets, just when it's absolutely essential he shouldn't be seen. Better get over there, do what has to be done and slip away before the next wave.

He's about to leave his hiding place when he detects movement opposite. Screwing up his eyes he sees that a child has emerged from the cellar. Cursing softly, the spy draws back into the shadows. His plan will work only if all three children are in the cellar with Sandra. As he watches, a second child appears, followed at once by a third. The trio stand on the rubble for a few seconds looking around, conversing in whispers. Then they split up and move off in three directions. Rags holds his breath as one of them passes the doorway that conceals him.

There are three important facts Rags doesn't know, and they could cost him his life. One: six children, not three, live with his assistant in the cellar. Two: at this moment one of those children is not in the cellar, nor is he one of those who have just emerged. Three: when that child, whom the others are searching for, returns to the cellar he will not come alone.

Ignorant of these facts, the spy can do one of two things: abandon his plan till tomorrow night and hope to surprise them all at home then, or wait and hope that the three children will shortly return. He knows tomorrow may well be too late, so he decides to wait.

As it turns out he's lucky, or at any rate he thinks he is. Ma has allowed Two Commando plus Wotsis to go look for Frecks on two conditions: that they confine their search to nearby streets, and that they return with all speed the second the ack-ack recommence firing. This happens less than five minutes later and Rags, caressing the gun in his pocket, smiles as he watches them reappear one by one and pop like frightened rabbits into their hole.

'*Zusammen,*' he murmurs, and smiles again adding, '*für immer.*'

Sixty-Five

'German spy ... *what* German spy? *Where?*' Cheese Roll's seriously hacked off with me, you can hear it in his tone.

I'm up on my feet by this time. I point northwest. 'Over there, Tooley Street, by Tower Bridge. He's got a second-hand clothes shop, there's a transmitter.'

Behind the corporal, his crew tinker with the light, conversing in subdued voices. He needs to get back to them, I know. 'Look,' I continue before he can come back at me, 'I know how it sounds: a kid's fantasy, right? Only it's not. It's *not*. There's a map – map of London – he puts red rings round places. Targets. After they're bombed he crosses 'em out. We've *seen* it – in fact we've got it at our place and the thing is, this site's on it: this searchlight, with a red ring. You're gonna be bombed, I came to warn you.'

He looks exasperated, shakes his head. 'Look, lad, the Hun don't need some *spy* to pinpoint a searchlight battery for him: when he's overhead, ours are the only lights he sees. We pinpoint *ourselves*, it's an occupational hazard and you've seen the consequences. So thanks for the warning, which I'd not be free to act on even if I believed your tale, which I don't, and if my light was operational, which it ain't. Now take yourself off to the nearest public shelter and leave me to get on with my job.'

He turns on his heel, leaves me standing like a dope, which I am in his eyes. I'm gobsmacked he thinks I'd lie: in fact I'm damn near crying, but anything I try to do now will only make things worse. Guns're starting up again in the distance, which means another wave of planes is on its way. I turn and run, back along the path, past the bandstand and out of the park. The streets are deserted, which isn't surprising. As I pelt from street to street I'm hoping two things: that I'll reach Victory Hall before the bombs start falling, and that my trousers'll have dried out a bit by the time I get there: I daren't *think* about what Nell'll say if they haven't.

As it turns out I don't make it, but it's not the bombs that stop me. I'm halfway down Fenner Road, the street we fetch water from, when some guy yells, 'Oi, you: where the bleat'n'ell d'you think you're going?' and these boots come pounding after me. Victory Hall's on the next corner but I mustn't lead him to it, whoever he is. I decide I'll have to run past and risk getting blitzed, but I'm right opposite when a heavy hand falls on my shoulder and I'm jerked to a halt.

'Now then, let's have a look at you.' He pulls me round to face him and I know him straight away. It's the policeman from the bandstand. He recognises me too. 'Blow me if it ain't the kid with the Yankee watch,' he pants. 'don't you *know* there's a raid on, son?'

I nod. 'Yeah, I know, but there's this spy . . .'

'*Spy?*'

He says it just like Cheese Roll so I don't know why I bother. I'm resigning myself to being frogmarched to some stinky shelter when I see something moving on the mound of rubble which covers Victory Hall. As I peer in that direction while trying to look as if I'm peering somewhere else entirely, a weak light clicks on over there, illuminating part of a face. I see a weak chin, a straggly moustache, the gleam of wire-rimmed glasses. 'It . . . it's *him*,' I croak, like someone in one of those detective series set in the Thirties.

The planes're practically overhead now, ack–ack going like mad, copper can't hear me. 'Eh?' He bends, cupping his ear, keeping a tight hold on me with his other hand.

I gesture towards Rags, who's doused his torch and is in the process of crawling under the chair. 'That's him, the *spy*.' I'm shouting. Doesn't matter *now* that I'm betraying the whereabouts of my friends. If Rags is here it can mean only one thing: he's found out we're on to him and means to silence us.

The officer looks where I'm waving, spots Rags, points his own hooded flashlight. The spy's on his knees. The racket's masked the noise we've been making, and he's been too intent on finding the way in to keep a lookout. He turns into the torchlight, one hand flung up to shield his eyes. In the other hand is a pistol.

When the policeman sees the weapon he relinquishes his hold on me, grabs his whistle and blows a series of long blasts. I'd forgotten they don't have radios: I doubt anyone's going to hear over the hubbub. He gives me a shove, mouthing something I don't catch – 'Stay back', probably – and moves towards Rags. I *can't* stay back, copper doesn't know my friends're under that rubble: he sees a guy with a gun, that's all. I follow. He's reached the foot of the mound when there's a whiplike crack, he crumples sideways and I'm within five metres of a killer with a smoking gun.

He's taking careful aim.

Sixty-Six

I freeze, eyes screwed tight. Born 1991, died 1940 goes through my brain, closely followed by a bullet. Except the bullet never comes. Instead a hefty constable hits me in the legs, knocking me over. At the same time a shape rises out of the rubble behind Rags and fastens itself to his neck. The spy topples forward with a cry, bringing Ma with him. Clamped together they start a slow downward slide in a shutter of bits and pieces.

It is obvious the copper isn't shot, the way he launches himself at Rags. The guy's hung onto his pistol in spite of Ma's piggyback ride. She dismounts and rolls clear as the two men grapple. 'All right, Frecks?' she pants. What a girl.

The planes have passed over us, flying north. Someone's getting it across the river. As I scramble to my feet two Home Guards come doubling along Fenner Street, presumably in response to the copper's whistle. I point at the wrestlers on the slope, yell, 'Watch it, he's got a gun!' and they close in, prodding Rags with the muzzles of their rifles. He's been scrapping like mad, but when he sees the soldiers he goes limp and lets the policeman pluck the weapon from his hand. Seconds later another constable arrives, then a third. They haul Rags upright, jerk his hands behind his back and snap on handcuffs.

The Home Guards lower their rifles, looking disappointed. 'Want us to shoot 'im?' asks one, hopefully. My policeman shakes his head.

I look at Rags in his dusty, crumpled suit. They're searching him, emptying his pockets. His hair, what's left of it, is mussed and there's a streak of dirt down his cheek. His glasses have slipped halfway down his nose and he can't push them up. If I didn't know he was an enemy agent facing execution, I'd take him for some poor downcast clerk caught with his hand in the till.

My constable's sprinted off to a police box somewhere, and as he reappears a car arrives with its headlamps shuttered and its bell ringing. The arresting officers help Rags into the back and one ducks in beside him, and that's the last I see of him.

Now the excitement's over the coppers're curious to know where all these kids've come from because they're all out: Nell, Wotsis and Mouse, Bertie and Siren. They know it's finished, their life at Victory Hall: you can see it in every face. Ma knows too, and she leads the way.

They stand amazed in the light from the Tilley lamps but they're the authorities: they've got their job to do. First it's names. Mouse won't do and Wotsis won't either: you can't jot down names like those in a little black notebook. They want Leonard and Armistead, and they need surnames as well. Mouse doesn't know what his surname is: he's forgotten it. The rest of us cough up. I try to think of it as us sacrificing our freedom that others might be free, but it's not easy. What the heck do I say when they want an address: *9 Cardigan Road, Witchfield, Year 2002*? I feel the loony bin looming.

Then something happens. Something stupendous. As the second policeman starts to question Ma, my constable plucks at the sleeve of my blazer and whispers, 'Hey, Georgie, give us one more shufti at that watch of yours, will you?'

Well, why not? Maybe he'll put in a good word for me at the local asylum. I shoot my cuff.

He gawps, points to a button. What's that for?'

'Gives you the date.'

'Never!'

'Does, watch.' I press. The time blinks out, and before the date has time to appear the constable blinks out too, and Victory Hall, and 1940. The very last thing I hear is Ma giving her name. 'Alexandra,' she murmurs: 'Alexandra Coverley.' Then I'm standing on the mound of pretend rubble in the 'Blitz' hut at Eden Camp with Miss Rossiter bellowing in my ear.

Sixty-Seven

'Where've you *been*, George Wetherall: we've had the place upside *down* looking for you.'

Where've I been? Now that's what I *call* a question. How do I answer? *Please, miss, I've been to nineteen-forty*, or *Please, miss, I've been to London*. Both true, but who's going to believe? Reckon I'd better settle for the dead-safe *Please, miss, I don't know*.

I don't give *any* of these answers. Fact is I'm so mind-blowingly, gob-smackedly glad to be back; so throat-achingly, eye-wateringly happy to see everybody, *including* Eve Eden, that I don't answer at *all*. Instead I fling my arms round Miss Rossiter like Ma grabbing Rags and burst out crying.

She's so embarrassed she doesn't know whether to comfort me or fight me off. 'It's all *right*, Georgie,' she twitters, twisting to get my bubbly nose off her neck. 'You shouldn't have wandered off like that but it's not the end of the world, for goodness' sake. We shan't be *expelling* you or anything like that.'

Everybody's gawping at us, kids and strangers alike. Some probably think we're part of the exhibit. BOMBED-OUT FAMILY IN EMOTIONAL REUNION. After a bit old Rossiter manages to break free without looking brutally insensitive and we leave the 'Blitz' hut. I gather we were all supposed to eat in the NAAFI canteen some time ago, but my disappearance has caused a postponement. As we hurry towards it now, I pluck at the teacher's sleeve.

'Miss, what *day* is this?' Well, I'm confused: I've been gone a fortnight and everybody's still here, rushing towards a two-week-old lunch. Won't it have got a bit *cold* by now? Won't our folks be wondering where the heck we've got to?

She looks at me like I'm some sort of nut. 'It's *Thursday*, George. It's been Thursday all day: it will remain Thursday until midnight, at which time we shall all be tucked up in our beds, unless of course you plan to disappear again – in which case who knows *when* we'll get home?

So it's like Scrooge. You know: *the spirits have done it all in one night*. I look at my watch. My so-called American watch. As far as I can tell, I ducked under that barrier just over an hour ago. A fortnight in an hour. I can feel a massive traffic-jam inside my skull: stuff to think about. Wonder about. To remember. It's all in there, gridlocked. It'll get sorted, it'll *have* to, only not now. Not yet.

For here's the NAAFI. The Navy, Army and Air Force Institute, I think it means. Inside I stop giving a stuff what it means, because the place is fat and fragrant with burgers and sausages and hot dogs and chips, and jelly and trifle and death by chocolate. There isn't a watery spud or a thin cabbage stew or a ration book in sight. Nobody's playing Snakes and Ladders in the light from a Tilley lamp, and nobody's dropping bombs.

It'll do for now.

Sixty-Eight

On the coach home I decide not to tell anybody. It's not a hard decision: nobody'd believe me if I did, and Pete and Danny'd laugh themselves sick. I don't know whether Rossiter'll grass me up to old Hollings for disappearing: he might take the view that it was her fault for not supervising me closely enough. Anyway, whatever happens I won't say anything.

Doesn't mean I intend forgetting everybody, I don't mean that. I *can't* forget – don't think I ever will. Nell. Bertie. Siren. Wotsis. Mouse. What became of them, I wonder, after I was snatched from among them? Were they split up, put in different homes? Did they survive the war, unlike Shrapnel, blown to bits: Spuggy, sliced in two? Is one of them still alive? Funny to think of them old.

Then there's Cheese Roll and my policeman and the two Home Guards. What happened to them? I wonder. They must all have wondered where I disappeared to.

And Rags: not Jewish at all, of course. A Nazi, but nobody's *idea* of a Nazi, just a sad, frightened little guy in wire-rimmed glasses who most likely was led out one damp morning into some bleak yard where six soldiers were waiting with rifles to shoot him through a paper target pinned over his heart. Such a lonely, unheroic end.

I've saved Ma till last on purpose. Brave Ma, fourteen years old, taking on a bunch of lost kids in the middle of a war. If it hadn't been for her we'd all have died – me fifty-nine years before I was born. Or would I never have *been* born? Too weird to think about.

You're probably way ahead of me, but in case you're not here's the twist. Ma and Miss Coverley turn out to be one and the same person. *Alexandra Coverley*, remember? Which means the gallant lass who took me in is the silly old bag whose garden I loved to wreck, and that's what time'll do.

Sixty-Nine

Time. Two weeks go by and it's still total gridlock in my brain. I haven't said a word to anybody about what happened to me, and Miss Rossiter can't have reported me to Hollings because I've heard nothing from him, but that doesn't mean everything's all right.

Don't get me wrong: it's great to be back. In fact I still can't believe my luck. I mean, I suppose if I'd operated the date function on my watch the day I arrived in 1940 I'd have come straight back and saved myself a lot of hassle, but on the other hand, what if I'd *lost* the thing? Had it smashed or stolen? Could easily have happened, and I'd be stuck there for ever. So I'm not moaning: I bless my luck every time Mum sticks a great plate of grub in front of me, and when I fall into bed and pull that cosy duvet up around my ears. All of that's absolutely terrific, but *this* is what I can't get my head round: across the road from our house there's Miss Coverley, who used to be Ma, and we share a mind-blowing secret.

Or *do* we? I mean, she says I remind her of someone and now I know who, but does *she*? How *can* she, when any sane person'll say it's impossible? *You're a time-traveller, aren't you, Georgie? Popped back to nineteen-forty and dropped in on the young me, didn't you, you rascal?*

Yeah, right.

Anyway, a fortnight goes by and it won't let me go. I guess I *know* what I'm going to have to do: talk to her. Bring the subject up, see if she's realised and if she hasn't, *tell* her. There's plenty of details I can mention: stuff I couldn't possibly know except by having been there. I can make her believe me all right, and then maybe I'll be able to put it behind me, get on with my life.

Snag is, I can't bring myself to do it. I set off once, marching across Cardigan Road, determined to confront her. *Morning, Miss Coverley, I was just wondering how the fence is holding up, and by the way d'you remember that coat you brought me, back in 'forty: made me look like George Raft?* Halfway across I come to a dead stop, mutter, 'No way', chicken out. It's worse than when Mum sent me across to apologise. Much worse.

Then one day the opportunity falls right into my lap. We're still doing the Home Front at school, and old Rossiter's wondering aloud if anybody's grandad or grandma happened to have been in London during the Blitz, because *that's* where it was all happening and it'd be super if he or she could come in and talk to the class about it. I'm bursting to say, *I was there myself actually*, but I'd get about three years' detention and more chewing-gum in my hair, so instead I shove my hand up and tell her I know an old lady who was in the Blitz. I figure if Miss Coverley comes in and talks about Victory Hall and the kids and I'm right there in front of her, it'll bring things to a head. She won't be able to prevent herself looking at me, and I'll stick in a question or two that'll put the issue beyond doubt. I might even find out what happened to the others.

Doesn't happen like that. I go over and ask her, which is hard enough, and she says yes, and I enquire after her fence which she tells me is holding up fine, but she doesn't let anything slip. Couple of days later there she is in front of the class, talking about her experiences in the Blitz, but I'm not in her story and she doesn't look my way. She mentions Mouse. Turns out he's alive and living in Wolverhampton and still drops her a line now and again. That's nice, but the nearest she comes to mentioning me is when she says sometimes in war people disappear and you never find out what happened to them. Doesn't glance at me even then, and I can't get it together to ask the questions I've prepared. Truth is, she's so cool I start wondering if any of it really happened or did I dream it all. War is mostly sad, she says.

When she leaves I ask to be excused and hurry after her along the corridor. I still don't know what I'll say but I know this is my last chance. If I don't speak now it'll stay bottled up for ever, doing weird things to my mind. She hears my footsteps and turns and it just comes out.

'Thanks for the George Raft coat, Ma.'

'That's all right, Frecks,' she says.

THE END

Activities

Additional support for using this novel in the classroom is available in the *Blitzed* Teaching and Assessment Pack. Including a CD-ROM and photocopiable resources, the pack contains lesson plans, video clips, images, resource sheets and an assessment task. To order a copy of the pack, please visit www.heinemann. co.uk/literature.

Alternatively, take a look at www.teachit.co.uk where you will find resources specially created for this novel.

Activity 1

Before reading

1 What does the word 'blitz' make you think of? Use a spidergram like the one below to record your thoughts.

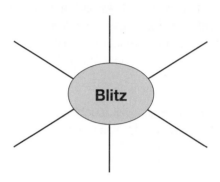

2 Use a thesaurus to look up the word 'blitz' and add more thoughts to your spidergram.

3 Make a poster or collage to show the different meanings or associations of the word.

4 Who or what do you think will be *blitzed* in this novel? What might this story be about?

5 Using the library or the internet, find out ten facts about the Blitz: when London was repeatedly bombed during World War II.

Activity 2

After reading Chapters 1–7

1   What are your first impressions of the way the narrator tells the story? Think about:

*   what the narrator describes
*   the way the narrator talks to the reader
*   the language the narrator uses
*   the tense the narrator uses.

   Try to comment on the effect of each of these on the reader.

2   By yourself, think of a word or two to describe Georgie and each member of his family. Find quotations from the novel to support your choices.

3   In pairs or small groups, draw a diagram of Georgie's family. Use labels, words, quotations from the novel and images to describe their characters, their interests and their relationships with each other.

4   Sometimes writers do not tell us about characters directly; they let the character's actions and words tell us about them. The reader has to *infer* what that character is like. Look at this quotation about Georgie's dad and the notes around it:

implies he is angry
with Georgie

'You're lucky to be setting off at all, lad, that crack about the Queen.'

implies respect for the royal family, and therefore traditional values as well, perhaps?

reinforces his anger – perhaps suggests a patronising attitude?

Now look at these quotations about Georgie's sister and his Mum. What can you infer about these characters from the writer's choice of language? Use notes, arrows and underlining to show what you can infer.

Georgie's mum:

'I don't think your sister's particularly interested in flying bombs, Georgie,' goes Mum, taking Em's hand. 'Come on, sweetheart, I know where there's some lovely ice-cream.'

Georgie:

I wouldn't ask her for a bucket of water if I was on fire, the miserable old bag.

Activity 3

After reading Chapters 7–11

1 Reread the last sentence of Chapter 7. What effect does the author intend to have on the reader? Can you find any other examples of this technique in the first six chapters?

2 Look again at Miss Coverley's last piece of dialogue in Chapter 7: 'You remind me of somebody...'. What effect does the author intend to have on the reader?

3 The chapters in this novel are very short. Why do you think the author has chosen this structure?

4 Look again at Chapters 7 and 9 and compare how Georgie's attitude to Miss Coverley changes. You will need to infer quite a lot from what Georgie says, thinks and does. Record your thoughts in a table like this:

	Chapter 7	Chapter 9	What this suggests
How he describes her			
What he says to her			
How he acts			

5 Write a paragraph describing someone you know. Try not to tell the reader what their character is like, but describe what they say, think and do so the reader can *infer* it.

Activity 4

After reading Chapters 12–18

1 Look again at the opening of Chapter 12. Why is the narrator trying to persuade the reader that his story is true?

2 How effective do you find the description of the time-slip? How could it have been written differently?

3 Why has the author used the device of a time-slip? If he wanted to write about the Blitz, why did he not use characters who were alive in the 1940s?

4 Why does the author emphasise how different this story is to other time-slip stories and films?

5 Look at the illustration at the start of Chapter 12. Compare it to the illustration at the start of Chapter 13. Why has it changed?

6 Working in a group, decide what you would do if you were in Georgie's situation. Try to come up with a five-point action plan: five ways in which you could get out of, or make the best of, your situation.

7 What do you think will happen next? By yourself or with a partner, think of three different ways in which this novel could develop and end.

Activity 5

After reading Chapters 19–23

1 Write a list of words or phrases which you think Georgie might use but would not be recognised by people in the 1940s.

2 Reread Chapter 19. Identify any language which is specific to the 1940s and is no longer used. Can you work out its meaning?

3 What kind of language is it that is no longer used? Why do you think this might be?

4 Reread Chapters 20–23, making a list of all the language specific to the 1940s. Use it to write a dictionary of 1940s English, giving definitions of all the words and phrases you find. You could look at an English dictionary to see what information you need to include and examples to help you write your definitions.

5 Working with a partner, design a presentation poster on 1940s English for display.

Activities

Activity 6

After reading Chapters 24–29

1 How does Georgie's behaviour in these chapters change your attitude to his character?

2 Why is it so important that Georgie's side do not win the game?

3 Write down three or four words to describe the character of Ma.

4 Find a quotation which supports each of the words you chose to describe her.

5 Try to explain *how* the quotation you chose supports your description of her character. You could record your thinking in a table like this:

Ma is...	Quotation	Page number	What the quotation suggests

6 Write down five questions you would like to ask Ma, then write down the answers you think she might give.

7 Working in a group, choose one person to play the role of Ma. Using some of your questions, interview Ma about her life and her experiences.

Activity 7

After reading Chapters 31–36

1   What are the important things in your life? Use a table like the one below to record them:

Games you play	Slang you use	Gadgets you use	Music: singers and songs	Food you eat	Clothes you wear	Traditions and beliefs

2   What historical details does the author include in these chapters to create the atmosphere of 1940's Britain? You could organise them in these categories:

Language	Music	Food	Games	Traditions	Beliefs	Clothes

3   Write a paragraph or two describing your day so far, or a recent weekend, trying to include as many of the details you gathered in question 1 to give a flavour of the times in which you live.

4   Look again at the paragraphs you have just written. Choose five words which you think you could improve or make more interesting. Try to think of three alternative words for each one. Decide which of the alternatives is better and will make the biggest difference to the vocabulary in your descriptive writing.

Activity 8

After reading Chapters 37–41

1   Reread Chapter 37. How many of these can you find in Swindell's descriptive writing: the five senses (sight, sound, smell, taste, touch); a simile, a list, emotive language, contrast?

2   Look back to the descriptive writing you did at the end of Chapter 36. How many of those techniques can you find in your own writing?

3   Read these two extracts taken from 1941 at the height of the Blitz:

'The British nation is stirred and moved as it never has been at any time in its long and famous history, and they mean to conquer or to die. What a triumph the life of these battered cities is over the worst that fire and bomb can do!'

Winston Churchill, broadcast 27 April 1941

'It has started! If they keep this up for another week, the war will be over. The East End won't be able to stand much more of this sort of thing. What's more, the Fire Brigade won't be able to stand much more of it either. This is the first leave I've had since Thursday…'

London Air Raid Warden, speaking in January 1941

Why do you think they give such a different picture of events?

4   Which one do you think is closer to the picture that Swindells describes in these chapters?

5   Stainer Street, London SE1 was actually bombed on 7 October 1940, killing 68 people. Does knowing this change the way you think about the events and characters in this novel?

6   Write a newspaper article about events in Stainer Street that night, using details from the novel. You could write it in the style of Winston Churchill, trying to keep your readers' spirits up – or you could make it much closer to the truth.

Activity 9

After reading Chapters 42–47

1 Reread the last three paragraphs of Chapter 45. What do you notice about the lengths of the sentences that the writer uses? What effect do you think he is trying to achieve at the end of this chapter?

2 Write one or two paragraphs of descriptive writing, trying to use a range of sentences to achieve the same effect as Robert Swindells. You could use one of these titles or one of your own:

- Entering the haunted house.

- Sneaking out of my house without being noticed.

3 Working in a group, decide what Georgie and Ma should do: tell the police about Rags and risk their group being broken up? Or keep quiet so that they can stay together? Try to think of two or three arguments on both sides before you make your final decision.

Activity 10

After reading Chapters 48–54

1   Read this sentence:

I _____ go to bed before ten o'clock.

Which of these modal verbs could go in the blank space?

- would
- could
- should
- might
- may
- have to
- ought to
- will
- shall
- must

2   What difference does the choice of modal verb make?

3   Reread the opening sentence of Chapter 48. Write a guide which will advise the reader: 'How to be a 1940s Child'. Skim read Chapters 48–54, and think back over your reading of the novel so far, to plan your writing. Examples of advice could include:

- what to eat – and how to get it
- what to do for fun
- how to talk to adults
- words to use
- how to catch spies.

Try to use modal verbs when writing your advice.

Activity 11

After reading Chapters 55–59

1   Reread the last sentence of Chapter 59. Once again, Swindells is creating a cliffhanger to hold the reader's attention and make them want to turn the page. Do a survey: how many of the 58 other chapters you have read so far end on a cliffhanger?

2   What are the qualities of an effective villain in a film or book? Write a list of ten things a villain should say, do or be.

3   Why do you think Robert Swindells decided to make Rags responsible for the deaths of civilians?

4   Why do you think he decided that Shrapnel should be killed in the bombing of Stainer Street? What does it make you think about Rags?

5   What else has the author done to make Rags an effective villain? Skim read Chapters 55–59 to find other details which the author has used. You could record your findings in a table like this:

What are we told about Rags?	Quotation	Why has the author done this?

Activity 12

After reading Chapters 60–63

1   In Chapter 61 the author tells us again about thieves who take advantage of the chaos caused by the Blitz. Why do you think he does this? How does it make you feel about the experience of living through the Blitz?

2   In Chapter 61 we are told that Georgie 'pees his pants'. Why do you think the author has done this? How does it make you feel about the character of Georgie?

3   In these chapters, the author uses a split or dual narrative: alternate chapters tell the story from two different points of view. Why do you think writers do this?

4   Look at the first sentences of Chapters 62 and 63; they are *in italics*. What purpose do these sentences have?

5   Think of an imaginary incident where it would be effective to use a split or dual narrative to tell the story. Storyboard the story, using alternate frames for the two different points of view.

Activity 13

After reading Chapters 64–66

1   What is the connection between Ma and Miss Coverley?

2   What does the word 'genre' mean?

3   Which different genres could *Blitzed* belong to? Try to think of two or three.

4   List the key features or ingredients of the genres you included in your answer to question 3. For example, some of the key ingredients of the ghost story genre are: a ghost, a spooky house, candles, strange noises, a dark moonlit night...

5   Decide which one genre you think best fits this novel. Write a paragraph explaining the features of *Blitzed* which helped you make this decision.

6   The author uses very little figurative language (similes, metaphors, etc.) and not much description in this novel. Why do you think this is?

7   It could be that description and figurative language are not the most important things in this genre of novel. What do you think *are* more important?

8   The cover of a book gives the reader a good idea of the genre of a novel. Design two new possible book covers for the novel, suggesting two different genres to the reader.

Activity 14

After reading Chapters 67–69

1 At the end of Chapter 64, Rags says something in German. Find out what this means translated into English.

2 What do you think Georgie has learnt by the end of this novel? Try to write a list of three or four different things. They could be things he has learnt about himself, or about the Blitz, or about how he thinks and behaves.

3 Some stories have a moral: a lesson or point that the writer wants the reader to learn. Think about how this novel's ending links to its beginning. What might be the moral of this story? Try to think of two or three possible answers.

4 Working in a group, compare all the possible morals you have thought of. Decide which one is most likely to be the point that the author wanted to make.

Activity 15

1 Write a description of one of the following:
   - Rags in prison
   - Ma and the other children waiting to hear from the police what will happen to them next
   - Georgie waiting outside his Head of Year's office, ready to explain what happened at Eden Camp when he disappeared.

   Try to create tension to keep the reader hooked and wanting to read on. Use effective description, a variety of sentences and try to end on a cliffhanger.

2 Which of the characters in the novel did you find most interesting and intriguing? Write an analysis of their character using the work you have done on the novel so far.

3 Now that you are an expert on the novel *Blitzed*, you have been hired as a consultant to help make the film version. Write notes for the director, the set designer, and the actors playing the parts of Georgie, Ma, Rags and Miss Coverley, explaining how they can make the film as good as possible.